My Story
BLITZ

VINCE CROSS

■ SCHOLASTIC

For my grandparents: Ella May and Bertie,
Isobel and William.

While the events described and some of the characters in this book may be based on
actual historical events and real people, Edie Benson is a fictional character,
created by the author, and her diary and its epilogue are works of fiction.

Scholastic Children's Books
Euston House, 24 Eversholt Street,
London, NW1 1DB, UK
A division of Scholastic Ltd
London ~ New York ~ Toronto ~ Sydney ~ Auckland
Mexico City ~ New Delhi ~ Hong Kong

First published in the UK by Scholastic Ltd, 2001
This edition published by Scholastic Ltd, 2014
Text copyright © Vince Cross, 2001
Cover photography © Jeff Cottenden, 2014

ISBN 978 1407 14610 2

Typeset by M Rules
Printed and bound by CPI Group (UK) Ltd, Croydon, CR0 4YY

2 4 6 8 10 9 7 5 3 1

The right of Vince Cross and Jeff Cottenden to be identified
as the author and photographer of this work has been asserted by
them in accordance with the Copyright, Designs and Patents Act, 1988.

Lewisham, London
1940

Saturday, 20th July 1940

I jumped out of my skin when the air-raid siren started wailing last evening. I was in the garden picking sweet peas for Mum and the whole bunch nearly went on the ground. It was very hot, even at seven o'clock, and there wasn't a breath of wind, the kind of weather that always makes you feel something's about to happen.

At tea Mum had been saying how rattled everyone seemed. That morning there'd been chatter at the shops. Someone knew for certain the Germans were going to invade this weekend, and they'd be in London by Monday unless our boys looked sharp. There are always rumours doing the rounds. It's difficult to know who to believe.

Anyway, Mum shouted from the kitchen for me to come in at once, sounding panicky. I wasn't going to argue. I couldn't see or hear any German bombers, but I've never been in an air-raid. How much time do you have between hearing a bomber fly over your house, and a bomb dropping and blowing you to bits?

As I went up the steps to go inside, I could see old Mrs Andrews from next door. She was walking in circles around her patch of lawn, looking up at the sky and wagging her finger, just like she was giving someone a good telling-off. God or the Germans? Who knows?

From inside our kitchen we could still hear her, the muttering turning into shouting.

"She'll get herself killed, she will," said Mum, sounding anxious and exasperated. "Barmy woman! Whatever's she doing?" Mum wafted me towards the hall. "You, go and get yourself under the stairs quick, while I try to sort Bessie out. As if life wasn't difficult enough!"

We're waiting for a proper air-raid shelter to be put in the garden. The Council's going to deliver one this week. In the meantime we're making do by sitting under the stairs or the kitchen table. It seems daft to me, but Mum says it's better than nothing.

I didn't do what Mum asked. I wanted to see what happened. I watched as she ran down the garden, out the back gate, and into Bessie Andrews's wilderness.

Old Bessie was drifting around in a world of her own. Mum might as well not have been there. Mum tried talking to her softly and when that didn't work she caught Bessie by the shoulders and shook her gently. The mad old woman pulled away and stared in complete amazement as if it was Mum who was off her head. I held my breath, wondering what I'd do if Bessie started hitting out. But she broke away in a sudden flood of tears and scuttled inside to her thirteen cats. Like Mum says, completely barmy!

4

Because it was Friday evening, and Dad was doing an extra shift at the Fire Station, no one else was at home, so Mum and I crouched together under the stairs listening to the wireless until, fifteen minutes later, the all-clear sounded. Just another false alarm!

Monday, 22nd July

When my sister Shirl crept out to go off to work this morning, I lay in bed for an extra half-hour. While the birds chirruped away merrily in the tree outside our window, all I could feel was miserable. It seems so muddled that there can be a beautiful blue sky and thrushes singing their heads off while there's a war with Germany going on, ships being sunk and people shooting at each other.

There's no one left to talk to, now that Maggie's gone. Alison left first, back in the panic last September. Lots of the children from my class at school were evacuated then, to Bexhill in Sussex. Mum says she can't think why they think it's safer there. If the Germans invade, it's the first place they'll arrive. Then, in May, Betty's parents got all nervous and packed her off to her Aunt Sally's in Devon.

5

Maggie's my best friend. She'd always said her family would never send her away, until last Friday she suddenly mentions casually she's off to Northampton till I don't know when. She might as well be going to the moon, as far as I'm concerned. So here I am all on my own-i-o, and feeling really fed-up and lonely, even if the sky is a wonderful clear blue.

That's why for the first time ever I've decided I'll keep a diary. I'm going to write down my real feelings about the awful, frightening war in this old exercise book. If I haven't got Mags, Alison or Betty to talk to, at least I'll have some way of giving vent to my thoughts and feelings.

Tuesday, 23rd July

So I'd better tell you about my family and where we live, hadn't I? I'll make a start with the house, and we'll get on to the people in a minute.

Summerfield Road runs beside a steep railway embankment about three-quarters of a mile from the town centre in Lewisham, and we live at number 47. It's all terraced houses round here, and I suppose our street is just the same as lots of others, except I like ours best. There are trees along the road, and you know you've arrived at our house because the front gate's painted bright green, Dad's favourite colour. Out the back there are lots of flowers and vegetables in a garden which goes down about 30 yards past the shed to the foot of the embankment. Every quarter of an hour during the day there's the long, loud rattle of an electric train on its way to Charing Cross. That's a big station right in the middle of London, eight miles away. Shirl and I are lucky to have a front bedroom. In the boys' room at the back it's far too noisy because of the constant clatter from the trains.

I often wonder what it was like when there really was a "summer field" where our house is now. It's funny to think of cows and sheep in our nice back garden. Perhaps that's why things grow so well. All that manure!

Anyway, now you know I've got a sister called Shirl, short for Shirley. She's much older than me. Seventeen and a bit full of herself, but she can be a good laugh. Considering we have to share, she doesn't get on my nerves *too* much. She works on the linen counter at Chiesman's department store in the centre of Lewisham, which is useful for us Bensons.

Tom's my little brother. He's ten, so he's very nearly two years younger than me. Tom can't keep still. There's always a streak of dirt showing on him somewhere. Unlike me, he doesn't read books unless he's forced to. What more can I say? He's a boy!

When Frank and Maureen were here, I had to share with

Tom, which was horrible with a capital H. Even so, I'd rather have Frank back. We all miss him terribly. I worry about him all the time and so do Mum and Dad. Frank is one of the ground crew at a Royal Air Force station called Biggin Hill. Everyone says he'll be safe and it's quite a cushy number, but how do they know? I'm sure the Germans are going to try to bomb the runways and planes Frank looks after. RAF pilots are killed every day now.

Frank's the oldest of us Benson children. Maureen's next and she's 21, but we don't hear from her much. She's with the army up north at some training camp. When she comes home, which is only once in a blue moon, she looks really smart in her khaki uniform, but I don't really know what she does. We've never got on, you see. Frank always brings me a present when he visits, even if it's just an old comic, but Mo just ignores me. Always has done!

My dad is Mr Albert Benson and he's wonderful. Nearly everyone calls him Bert. I think I told you he's a fireman, and he's as big and strong as you'd expect a fireman to be. He doesn't get cross very often (and never with me) though Mum makes up for it. She's nice underneath, but she hides it well by shouting a lot. I think she does the worrying for too many people, though maybe it's just her red hair. Mum's name is Beatrice, which sounds a bit old-fashioned to me. Don't tell her I said so!

So there you are! Now you know all about us. Oh, I nearly

forgot. I'm Edie, short for Edith (ugh!). Pleased to meet you, I'm sure.

PS I mustn't leave out Chamberlain, our fox terrier! I know it's a funny name, but Dad says it's because he's always hopeful, just like the old Prime Minister. That was Mr Neville Chamberlain who thought he could make peace with the Germans. He was the one who came before Mr Churchill. Our Chamberlain's usually disappointed too! I suppose if we ever had a bulldog, he'd be called Churchill. You can tell from looking at his face Mr Churchill won't take any nonsense from Jerry.

Thursday, 25th July

You know that lovely back garden I was telling you about? Well, it doesn't look half as neat and tidy as it did a day or two ago.

Frank came home on leave yesterday afternoon. He's got a motorbike down at Biggin Hill, and he managed to wangle some petrol, even though it's not really allowed because of the rationing. He looks just *so* wonderful and romantic in his uniform, though Dad didn't let him keep it on two minutes.

No sooner was Frank through the front door than the two of them were in the garden digging the hole for our new air-raid shelter. Now we'll be safe no matter what Hitler tells his bombers to do!

Mind you, Dad was a bit fed-up when he found out he'd have to buy our safety. He had to shell out seven quid for the shelter, and apparently all because he earns *too much*. First I've heard! Most people in the street have got theirs free. It's called an *Anderson* shelter after the man who thought it up, and the first thing you have to do is dig this hole.

You should have seen the size of it. I said it looked as if they were tunnelling to Australia, and Frank said it felt as if they were. The hole's three feet deep, and of course it's got to be long and wide enough for us all to sit inside. Dad and Frank bolted together the corrugated iron sheets to make the roof and sides, and finally they piled all the earth back on to the top, deep enough that you could grow rhubarb. Dad says that's what we're going to do. Fancy spending the night under a clump of rhubarb! Anyone would think we were a family of rabbits – still, at least we'll be safe rabbits! When they'd finished, Tom and I lit a candle, and crept inside. It felt really cold and spooky, but I suppose when we're all in there together it won't be so bad.

I'm a woodenhead. I told you my name the other day, but afterwards I realized you don't know anything else about me. Well, I'm tall for my age (about five-foot-three), and I'm skinny, and in summer I get awful freckles all round my face. Mum says I'd be clever if I put my mind to it, but I don't know about that. I look a lot like Shirl, but I don't think I'll ever be as pretty. (Mind you, she spends long enough doing her face!) I like going to the pictures, I like books, and I'm good at netball. I'm as good as Tom at football too, but you'd better not tell him. Oh, and I *hate* rice pudding, which is a pity because Mum makes one every Sunday dinnertime. All that sloppy milk with bits in. Ugh!

Saturday, 27th July

Mum's been like a cat on hot bricks since Frank's visit. I caught her moping in the kitchen after he'd roared off down the road towards Bromley. She said Frank had told her bad things.

Apparently there's German aircraft in the skies over Kent every day now, trying to take pictures, and Frank says it's only a matter of time before they try to shoot up the airfields. After that he thinks they really will start bombing London.

Building the Anderson has made it all seem so much more real. Dad's taking it more seriously too. He checked all our gas masks last night and made Tom and me practise putting them on, in case Hitler puts poison gas in the bombs. When you look in the mirror, it's like there's a monster or a creature from outer space looking back at you.

Then after dark we tried out the shelter. Dad's made it as comfortable as possible with a bit of old carpet laid across the planks, but it's cold and clammy even on a nice warm and dry July evening. Whatever's it going to be like when it rains and it's the middle of winter? As soon as we got in there, Tom decided he wanted to go to the toilet. Mum tutted and said he should have thought of that earlier. That's all very well, but what if we're in the shelter for hours, and the bombs are falling? What do we do then? Run inside the house and go as quickly as possible, I suppose. Dad won't have time to read the newspaper like he usually does!

Tuesday, 30th July

What a cheek! I know Mr Churchill, the Prime Minister, says we've got to "dig for victory", because Britain needs to grow more food, but digging up the Lewisham municipal park's going a bit far! Where am I going to walk Chamberlain now?

12

I said to Dad I couldn't see the point, what with it being July. There wasn't anything they could plant. Dad said he reckoned they'd put in allotments and everyone would grow cabbages. Wonderful! So not only is the park going to look horrible, it's going to smell awful too. Not fair!

Shirl's got herself a boyfriend at last. I'm sure she has. If not, who was the bloke who walked her home after work last night?

Friday, 2nd August

The strangest thing happened yesterday, really frightening. It's getting dark slightly earlier again now, and when I went up to bed at about nine o'clock there wasn't enough light to read. Shirl needed to take off her warpaint and we had two candles lit in the room so we could both just about see without having the electric on. Anyway, we mustn't have drawn the curtains properly, because five minutes later there's a huge knock on the door like the world's coming to an end and when Mum answers it she finds a policeman on the doorstep making a fuss. Then he elbows his way past her into the house, saying someone's signalling to the Germans.

Mum tells him as politely as she can that he must be off his rocker, but he demands to see our room and waltzes upstairs to give us a right bawling out, shouting didn't we know there was a blackout and were we on Jerry's side? Shirl was completely shocked and embarrassed, and I cowered under the eiderdown. Good job Shirl still had most of her clothes on!

When he'd finally gone Mum went completely mad. She didn't know whether to be more annoyed with us for showing her up, or with him for being so rude and barging in like that. Shirl and I ended up in tears and all in all it was a horrible end to the evening. When Dad came home at the end of his shift this morning, Mum packed him off down the police station to tell the desk sergeant what he thought, but I don't see what good that'll do.

I suppose the blackout's necessary. It makes sense that we shouldn't give the Jerry bombers any idea of what's on the ground, but it doesn't half cause problems. Dad said it was a good thing it was only a beat copper and not one of the ARP wardens who usually go round telling people to put lights out, because they really *are* little dictators. Then Mum shocked us all by saying that if you can't beat 'em you should join 'em, and that she thought she'd apply to be a warden, because none of them had two grains of sense to rub together and if things got really nasty we couldn't afford to leave it to morons. So that'll be four of the family with uniforms, five if you include what Shirl has to wear for Chiesman's. Shirl said I could always join the girl guides if I was so desperate. I told her she must be joking. No uniform was worth that!

Tuesday, 6th August

You've got to hand it to Mum. If she says she's going to do something there's no stopping her. Yesterday she went down and signed up as an ARP warden, just like she'd said. No uniform, though. Just an arm-band with ARP (for "Air Raid Precautions") written on it in big white letters.

Dad laughed when he saw her. "We're all in trouble now, Beattie," he said. "Signed up just like that! How do they know you aren't a German spy?"

"Sid Bazeley's running the show down there," Mum answered, unpinning her hat. "If he doesn't know I'm not a spy, there's something wrong. We were kids together in Madras Terrace. There's a few stories I could tell you about Sid!"

Ever since Shirl and I had our spot of bother last week, Mum's been flapping about the blackout. She checks our room every evening, and makes us pin up spare blankets round the window.

"Now it won't matter what you two monkeys get up to," she says.

I suppose if she's going to be a warden and boss other people about, she's got to keep things tight at home.

The warden's post is in our old school, down Hengist Road. They moved in as soon as the kids were evacuated last year. There hasn't been any proper school since, because all the teachers were evacuated as well, and it's funny to think of the wardens sitting in our old classrooms drinking tea. Mum says it's about time the ARP did something more for people than just shouting at them. She's got ideas about running concerts, and parties for the kids and all that. We'll see. From what I remember of Sid Bazeley, it's not the kind of thing he'd go for. He keeps a fruit and veg shop up towards Catford and he's always been as miserable as sin with us kids.

As far as the blackout goes, there's good news and bad news. You'd be surprised at the number of accidents that happen because no one can see anything in the dark. Last week in Dad's local paper I read that someone was killed falling off a railway platform over near Bromley. And just down the road old Annie Makins toppled off the kerb one night and broke her ankle, poor thing! In some places they're painting the kerbs white, and even putting a white band round postboxes so that you don't walk into them, but they haven't got to Summerfield Road yet.

The good news? You should just see the stars! In the old days before the war they were always hidden by the street lights. Now on clear evenings the sky's jet-black and covered with millions of sparkly diamonds. You can even see the Milky Way stretching across like a sort of gauzy scarf.

Wednesday, 7th August

I'm really bored. It's raining and it doesn't feel like the summer holidays one bit. But then since there's no school terms now, what's a holiday and what isn't?

When everyone was evacuated last year, it was great at first. As I said, all the teachers went off with the kids, and there wasn't anyone left to run the schools so we had to stop at home. But I really didn't want to be packed off to Sussex or Devon or somewhere where we wouldn't know anybody, and I could see Tom was scared stiff too. I got myself in a right state worrying till finally Mum said they'd send Tom and me away over her dead body.

Mrs Chambers from the school paid us a visit to try to make her change her mind. I was listening outside the front parlour door and there was quite a row. Mrs Chambers said Mum was setting a bad example. She ought to do what the government said was best. Mum said she didn't like anyone telling her what to do when it came to her children. Mrs Chambers snapped: what would Mum feel like if a bomb dropped and Tom and me were killed?

Mum didn't say anything for a moment. I put my ear right to the keyhole and heard her whisper that if we were, she hoped we'd all go together, and she wasn't going to give in to threats from Hitler or Mrs Chambers, thank you. And that was that.

So, most of this year, Tom and me have spent three mornings each week with Mrs Riley. She used to be a teacher until she retired. Mrs Riley's very nice, but it's not like school. For starters she has trouble staying awake a whole morning, and though she's all right at reading and writing, I know more about geography than she does. Tom isn't interested at all. It's all Mrs Riley can do to keep him in his seat for ten minutes at a time, he's such a shufflebottom. I read with him a bit each day and give him a few sums to do. The rest of the time I help Mum, and do as many paper rounds as I can for Mr Lineham. He owns the corner shop.

So you see I miss school, and my friends. Especially when it's raining like it is today!

The same bloke walked Shirl home again last evening. Looks a bit old for her, if you ask me! And he's got a moustache. I won't ask Shirl if it tickles!

Saturday, 10th August

Yesterday was my birthday. I can't quite believe I'm twelve. I keep saying, "Edie Benson is twelve years old!" to myself. I think it sounds much better than eleven, don't you?

Mind you, it was a funny start to a birthday. We were all in the Anderson half of Thursday night. The sirens went at nine in the evening and then again somewhere around midnight, so we were all a bit bleary-eyed by the morning. There's still no bombs, leastways not that we've heard. I wonder what it's going to be like when they do start falling?

In Mum's *Woman's Own* the "Doctor's Note" column says if you want to sleep at night you should eat lots of lettuce and nothing at all in the evenings. Oh, and cotton wool ear plugs are supposed to help too. I bet the Doctor doesn't spend his nights with four other people in a hole the size of a rabbit hutch! Is that why rabbits eat lettuce? To help them sleep?

There was a lovely surprise at tea-time. Maureen had got some leave and turned up on the doorstep with a big bunch of flowers for Mum, and a really nice hair-band for me. Fancy that! I'd been secretly hoping Frank would get home too, but at least he remembered to send a card to his "favourite not-so-little sister".

In the evening we all went off to the Lewisham Hippodrome to see *Over the Rainbow*, with me feeling very grown up about going out to the theatre of an evening. Even Dad managed to wangle out of a shift to come with us. *Over the Rainbow* is the Wizard of Oz story, just like the film with Judy Garland that everyone's talking about. It was so funny and sad and beautiful, and even though we were sitting right up at the back it was a wonderful treat for a special day. Best of all, we got right through the evening without an air-raid warning, so well done Frank and the lads in the RAF. They must have scared the bombers away just for me. By the time we'd walked back to Summerfield Road we were all properly done for, what with the lack of sleep from the previous night.

One of the things I miss about school is not being in plays. I'd really, really like to be Dorothy in the *Wizard of Oz*. Last night I just wanted to jump up on stage and sing along.

Sunday, 11th August

Today was Civil Defence Day in Lewisham, and of course Mum had to be on duty along with all the other wardens. Dad was working, and went out grumbling. They'd all been told to turn up with their shoes shined and their uniforms smartly pressed. "Someone important" was coming to inspect them. "Don't they know there's a war on?" he muttered. "We've got more than enough work to do, without standing around waiting for la-di-da rubberneckers."

Shirl had gone off to Chiesman's at about half past seven, so when Tom and I'd done the breakfast dishes and got the house more or less straight (well I had!) we sneaked out to see what was going on.

Until we talked about it the other evening, I hadn't cottoned on that Mum's going to be right in the thick of things if the bombs do start falling. When a factory or a house gets hit the wardens are supposed to get there as quick as they can. They take a quick shufti and then they've got to telephone the Town Hall to tell the ARP centre what's happened. How many people have been hurt or killed? Is anyone still trapped

21

in the rubble? Then they do what's necessary, rescuing people and giving first aid until proper help arrives.

Mum's very brave. It made me shudder to think about finding dead bodies and things. I don't think I could do it.

Down by Finch's Builders' Yard there was a crowd gawping at something, but we couldn't get close enough to see. Tom amazes me, really he does. He knows the alleys and back doubles much better than me, and eventually he found a wall we could sit on with a view out over the yard.

Everyone was pretending a bomb had just fallen. We couldn't see Mum but various wardens were running around like scalded cats. There were people lying on the ground. They were groaning loudly and waving their arms and legs to show they were injured until nurses came and bandaged them up. None of them would have won any prizes for acting. Then they were stretchered off into a couple of ambulances. After five minutes of this Tom was already saying, "I've had enough," so we jumped down from the wall and walked on into Lewisham. Occasionally we could hear the bells on the fire engines ringing, so we headed for the Fire Station, me trying to keep up with Tom.

"Just make sure Dad doesn't see us," I shouted at his heels. "We'll catch it if he does, especially today!" Dad doesn't like us hanging around the Station. "Work and home?" he says. "Oil and water!"

The crowd around the Fire Station was huge, so this time

there was nothing for it but to push to the front. There was a lot of excited chatter.

"Let the littl'uns through," said a big lady wearing a pink and yellow headscarf who was looming behind us. "They'll want to see royalty." As the crowd parted, she shoved us forward, using us as the excuse for her to get a better view too.

I turned my head and asked her, "What royalty?" and over the crowd's cheering she shouted, "It's the King and Queen, ducks! Come to see how the other half lives!"

In front of us we could see a line of firemen standing against a gleaming fire engine, while with their backs to us a man in smart military uniform moved slowly down the line accompanied by a lady in a blue feathered hat. We were just in time to see them pass Dad. The King stopped and seemed to say something, and Dad bowed his head slightly, smiling a reply.

"It's not the King!" said Tom a bit too loudly. "Where's his crown?"

"Don't be so daft," I said. "You don't think he carries it with him everywhere, do you?" Tom tutted. "You're the end, you are," I said. "Here's your dad meeting the King, and all you care is that he's not wearing the Crown Jewels on his head."

A few minutes later, the King and Queen shook the mayor's hand and sped off in shiny black cars towards Blackheath. Then there were some rescue demonstrations with people jumping off the Fire Station tower into sheets, and firemen showing how to put out pretend incendiary bombs – the little ones that don't blow you up, but just burn you to death by starting fires. Apparently you don't throw water over them like everyone thinks. That only makes things worse. You have to use sand. I think Tom enjoyed that more than seeing the King.

"Funny thing about that inspection, Beat. . ." Dad said to Mum later at tea.

"I know," she said. "I heard. Didn't come to see us workers, did they?" She sounded miffed, but she was only joking. Proud really.

"Spoke to me, he did," said Dad, looking round at us all. "Our King spoke . . . to *me*."

Dad had us in the palm of his hand. We were holding our breath waiting to hear details of this great conversation.

"Do you want to know what he said, then?"

We all nodded our heads. Dad pulled his mouth wide, showed his teeth and put on a high-class accent, " '*Isn't it a laavely day*'."

"Bert!" said Mum.

"He did!" said Dad. "Come to Lewisham to cheer us up, and talks about the weather. I ask you! I feel so much better now!" He shook his head.

"At least he came!" said Mum. "They could just hide away in a bunker, you know!"

Monday, 12th August

Mum sprung something on us today. She's taking Tom and me to see Auntie Mavis down near Tonbridge tomorrow. Yippee! And we're staying till Friday. It's a holiday, or at least something like it.

No beach, but at least we'll be out of smelly Lewisham. (And getting smellier all the time! Now they're letting people keep *pigs* in their back garden and they've put waste bins on the street corners. The idea is we should put all our old food scraps in them to feed the wretched porkers. And when it's as hot as it was yesterday, you don't want to go nearer than half a mile to those bins. They stink to high heaven!)

Shirl's in a right sulk about Tonbridge. She scarcely spoke to me all evening. I think she fancied a few days in the country.

When we were getting ready for bed, I asked her about the bloke who walks her home. She blushed red to her roots. Very satisfactory!

"What's his name?" I asked.

"Mind your own business!" Shirl snapped. Then, because she was clearly dying to tell someone, she gave in. "Oh go on!

It's Alec, if you must know. I think he's a bit sweet on me."

"And you?" I pushed.

"Mind your own business!" she said again. And this time the shutters were down. For the time being. . .

Tuesday, 13th August

We caught a bus down to Hither Green and didn't have to wait long for the electric train to Sevenoaks. That was where the fun and games started.

When you get to your destination these days, you have to hope you hear the porter shout "Sevenoaks" or whatever the station is because there aren't any signs. They've all been taken down. Dad says the idea is that if the Germans ever do invade, they won't know where they are. It's the same with road signs.

Luckily that wasn't a worry because our train was only going as far as Sevenoaks. Then we sat and waited for ages for the steam train to take us on to Tonbridge. Tom didn't mind. I can't think why, but he actually likes standing on station platforms watching engines shunting backwards and forwards.

"Flippin' war!" said a man standing next to us. "Gives them all the excuse they need, don't it? Blessed trains don't never run to time now."

Eventually a train puffed into a platform on the far side of the station. We ran over the footbridge in a panic. No one seemed to know if it was the Tonbridge train, and even when we finally set off, Mum was still a bit nervous, asking the other passengers if we were all going to end up in Hastings.

Inside the trains now there are blinds on every window so it's really dark. It's the blackout again. A brightly lit train would be a sitting target at night I suppose. There are strange blue lamps in all the compartments so that you can just about see, though only so as not to fall over each other.

We were two hours late arriving in Tonbridge, but little Uncle Fred – red cheeks polished and shining under a cheeky hat – was still there waiting for us. With his car.

"We could have caught the bus," said Mum. "Think of the petrol. You don't want to waste your rations."

Uncle Fred tapped his nose. "No names, no pack-drill," he said. "Never a problem with a bit of extra petrol, if you know where to ask."

Mum pretended to look shocked. Then: "How's Mavis?" she asked. I glanced over at Tom. The way she asked the question, it wasn't just a polite enquiry, she was really concerned. But Tom hadn't noticed anything.

"The old girl's not so well. Not at all," Uncle Fred answered, and I could have sworn he blinked rather more than he should've.

Of course as soon as we actually saw Auntie Mavis I knew why we'd come to Tonbridge all of a sudden. She seems half the size I remember, and her skin's a sickly kind of yellow colour. This might be a holiday for us, but I'm afraid Mum's visiting her sister for quite another reason.

Wednesday, 14th August

When we got a moment to ourselves this morning, I asked Mum about Auntie Mavis. She looked me straight in the eye.

"She's very ill, Edith," Mum said softly. I always know something's up when she calls me by my full name like that. "We've just got to look after her as much as we can. And Fred. I don't know what he'd do without Mavis." And she turned away rather too quickly.

In the afternoon Tom and me walked out through the houses into the fields. We climbed up steadily towards a wood, the corn as high as Tom's shoulders on both sides of the path. We were almost level with the trees when we heard the first planes, high and distant. We turned and looked, shading our eyes against the sun.

"There," said Tom, pointing into the sky. It took me a

couple of moments but then I saw them too, a formation of dots dodging the clouds.

"Germans," Tom added.

"Do you think so? How do you know?" I asked.

"Heinkels! You can tell by the shape, can't you?" he said, like I was just a stupid girl and knew nothing. But he was right, because then there was the sound of more planes coming from behind us over the wood, and as the German bombers came nearly overhead, suddenly the sky above us was full of aircraft zooming up and down, and we began to hear gunfire.

I don't know about Tom, but I was rooted to the spot. I'd never seen or heard anything like it, and it was all so sudden and unexpected. I didn't know whether to run for home, or take shelter in the woods.

"What do we do, Tom?" I asked, though I should have been making the decision myself.

He just shrugged his shoulders. "Stay and watch?" he suggested.

So we did. It seemed like the dogfight went on for hours, but it was probably more like ten minutes. We saw one plane start to smoke as it wheeled away from the pack. Then it seemed to hang and pitch forward, before tumbling over itself into a dive that took it out of sight to the side of a hill. It must have fallen miles away, because there was no sound of its landing, no explosion.

"I hope it was one of theirs," said Tom, almost enjoying the moment.

"The pilot might be dead," I replied, not sure what to think.

"Good!" said Tom. "The only good German is a dead. . ."

"Shut up," I said. "You mustn't say that."

"Why not?" he asked crossly. "It's true."

Tom and I don't fall out very often, but after that we walked in silence for a bit. As we crossed the road towards Auntie Mavis and Uncle Fred's house there was shiny metal lying on the concrete.

"Bullets," said Tom, eyes wide with excitement. He went to pick one of them up.

"Don't you dare," I shouted. "You might blow your hand off. Stop, Tom. Now!"

He gave me a dirty look, but he did as he was told.

So that's it. Now the war's real. It's happening to us, not just to other people.

Thursday, 15th August

The first thing you notice about living in Tonbridge is how quiet it is. So when the telephone rang in the middle of last night, I almost jumped out of my skin. There's no telephone at Summerfield Road. It's a call box for us if we ever want to talk to Auntie Mavis or Uncle Fred. Telephones in houses are posh, I reckon.

Uncle Fred works near Sevenoaks at somewhere called Fort Halstead. I know he works for the Government, but that's all I know, and Mum says it's probably best not to ask. Uncle Fred's definitely clever. You only have to play him at chess to know that. Dad says he's a boffin, whatever that is.

The telephone hadn't wakened Tom. He was breathing deeply, still fast asleep. I pulled a jumper over my nightie and gently opened the bedroom door. I could hear Uncle Fred talking into the phone down in the hall. I tiptoed across the landing as he said goodbye to whoever was on the other end of the line. As he put the phone down, he turned and saw me at the top of the stairs and it was his turn to jump. There was a strange look on his face, half amused, half worried.

"What's the matter, Uncle Fred?" I whispered, coming down the stairs and sitting on the bottom step.

He looked at me as if he couldn't decide what to say. "It's probably nothing," he stalled.

"It can't be nothing," I insisted. "Not in the middle of the night!"

He gave in. "All right. I'm a member of the Home Guard, Edie love," he whispered back. "And people are always seeing things. Somebody reckons the Germans have landed out

Paddock Wood way. It's a load of baloney, of course. It's probably just a poacher, but I'll have to go and make sure. Look, it's more likely to be Martians than Germans, so go back to bed and don't worry."

I hadn't seen the rifle hidden behind the hat-stand in the hall until then.

Back upstairs, I heard his car drive off, and for the next two hours I lay and shivered, half-expecting a brigade of stormtroopers to smash their way in though the front door. But when he came back, he shut the door behind him so gently and carefully I knew we hadn't been invaded by either Martians or Germans, and I rolled over and went to sleep.

This morning we caught a bus into Tonbridge, and went shopping for Auntie Mavis. When she makes tea it normally comes out a thick dark brown colour. "Strong enough to stand a spoon up in," Mum says. She must use about five teaspoonfuls. But now they're rationing tea just like they do butter and meat. To get your ration you have to hand in coupons from your ration book. So if we come down again, maybe Auntie Mavis's tea will be drinkable!

If we come down again! According to Mum what poor Auntie's got is cancer, and the doctors don't give her much chance. What does *that* mean? Months? Weeks?

Poor Mavis. Poor Mum. Whatever does it feel like to know your sister is dying of cancer? It could be me and Shirl!

Friday, 16th August

At breakfast, while Mum was helping Auntie Mavis make the porridge, I asked my uncle, "What's it like in the Home Guard, Uncle Fred?"

He twinkled at me. "It's all right. Makes me feel young again."

"Why's that?" I asked.

"Everybody else is older than me, that's why," he laughed. "And don't look so amazed!" He pulled a face. "All right, maybe I'm exaggerating but there *are* a fair few old codgers in our company. George Chapman must be 65 if he's a day. But we've all got to do our bit, haven't we?"

"What *do* you actually do, then?" piped up Tom.

"Well, they're training us to guard anything strategically important – gun batteries, railways, main roads, all that kind of thing. If Hitler was daft enough to invade, we'd do our best to make life difficult for him."

"Is it true you've only got broomsticks and pitchforks to fight with?" Tom asked. He hadn't spotted the gun either. I don't think Tom meant to be rude, but that's the way it sounded, and I kicked him hard. I needn't have worried though. Uncle Fred was laughing.

"Not quite. When we first enrolled about four months ago, it's true there weren't many weapons available. But they're working us hard now. We'll even have a machine gun soon!"

"How do you find the time?" I said.

"Oh, it's not so bad. There's plenty of evenings and weekends." He looked me straight in the eye, and dropped his voice. "Takes my mind off things, to be honest."

"Have you ever thrown a grenade?" asked Tom enthusiastically.

"Only pretend ones," said Uncle Fred. "Hope I never have to throw one for real. Still, I was a good cricketer at school! I expect it'd be all right."

"Do you think it's true the Germans would use poison gas?" I asked. I have bad dreams about the gas. In them I'm always trying to escape from Summerfield Road. However hard I struggle, my legs won't carry me out of the house. I can't see anything and I can't breathe.

"Depends how you look at it," said Uncle Fred, leaning back in his chair. "On the one hand it's against the rules of war. And on the other hand I wouldn't put anything past that dreadful little man if he found himself in a tight spot."

Then Mum and Auntie Mavis came into the dining room. Uncle Fred stopped talking, like turning off a tap, and turned and smiled at Auntie as if there wasn't anything to worry about in the whole world.

Saturday, 17th August

Until we got home, I hadn't realized how much I'd missed Summerfield Road. Lewisham isn't so smelly after all! (Well it is, but no worse than Tonbridge. Pigs in the one, cows in the other!)

And it seems ages since we went away, although it's really only five days. It's funny the things you notice for the first time. A pile of sandbags on a street corner here, a roll of barbed wire there. You can't be sure, but you don't think they were there a few days ago. It's as if, week by week, water's building up pressure behind a dam and sooner or later it's going to burst. Does that make sense?

Dad seemed to have survived Shirl looking after him. But the big wide grin on his face when we walked through the front door showed how pleased he was to have us back. He almost swung my mum off her feet and gave her a great big kiss.

"Put me down, Bert," she said. "Go on with you. Everybody knows it's only the apple pie you miss."

It's funny to see them like that, and it made me extra sad to think about Auntie Mavis and Uncle Fred.

Chamberlain was glad to have us back too. I hope they've been feeding him properly.

Tuesday, 20th August

I was reading Dad's *Kentish Mercury*, catching up on last week's news, and there's something I don't understand.

If Hitler and the Nazis are so bad, like most people say, why are there some people who don't agree?

Apparently there was a Communist demonstration against the war down in Catford on Wednesday. I asked Dad about it and he said the police actually stopped some men who wanted to give the Communists a bloody nose.

"I don't see why," I said. "They're traitors."

Dad looked serious for a minute. I thought I'd made him cross, though I didn't know the reason.

"It's what we're fighting for, girl," he said. "There's no free speech in Germany. If your face doesn't fit, you're for the high jump. That's why our Frank's spending the best years of his life in a dirty God-forsaken hut down at Westerham. And our Maureen, wherever she is up north. Don't ever forget, it doesn't matter what someone's opinions are, they've a right to speak their mind."

I still don't get it.

Wednesday, 21st August

And here's something else from the paper. Every week there's a sort of court called a tribunal where conscientious objectors have to go to explain why they don't want to fight. This time it was someone who said he was a Christian pacifist, and he was about to go to Bible College.

From what I can see they let him get away with it. They've put him on "non-combatant duties only", and I reckon he was just spinning a yarn. Mum agrees and says in the Great War the girls used to hand out white feathers to men who wouldn't fight to show them they thought they were cowards. But Mum said she thought "non-combatant" only meant he wouldn't have to fire a gun. He might still end up in the front line carrying stretchers.

Then later I started thinking about what it would feel like to be "called up", and how frightened I'd be if it was me.

But they've still got to do their duty, haven't they? Frank and Maureen are! I just wish they didn't have to.

Meanwhile Shirl is having a high old time. She was out with Alec again last night. Up at the Palais, dancing till gone 10.30. I saw the looks Mum and Dad exchanged when she went out done up to the nines – lipstick, stockings and all.

"Is that our daughter, Beat?" said my father. "Pretty as a picture, isn't she?"

"If you say so," Mum answered, lips pursed and hand on hip. "I hope she knows what she's doing!"

Interesting!

Tuesday, 27th August

There I was queuing for bananas at the greengrocer's, when suddenly there was a tremendous kerfuffle on the other side of the road, and everyone in the queue turned to look. Two men were holding another one in an armlock. They seemed to be trying to frog-march him down towards the clock tower, till a copper came up and stopped them. Then there was a lot of shouting and fingerpointing, and the one man kept trying to throw punches at the other two. The policeman's helmet went on the skew over his eyes, and people started sniggering.

Rosa Jacobsen, who used to go to my school, was trailing down the pavement watching what was going on.

"Watch'er Rosa," I said. "What's that all about?"

"They think he's a fifth columnist or something," Rosa answered.

That was a new one on me. "And what's that when it's at home?"

"Like a German spy who's been living here and doing sabotage. Blowing things up and that!"

"So how come they're so sure?" I asked Rosa.

She shrugged her shoulders. "I dunno," she said, disappointed now no one was hitting anyone else. "Spoke with an accent, I expect."

That rang bells. The *third* thing I'd read in the *Kentish Mercury* was about a priest called Schwabacher (or something like that). Till last week he'd been working up at a church in Blackheath for years, but now he's been sent off to an internment camp, like a prison, just because his dad was German.

Surely a priest wouldn't be a spy, would he? The world's getting more confusing every day.

I expect you're wondering about the bananas. It's funny, but no one in our house would touch a banana before the war. Now a rumour goes around that Harrold's had a few boxes of them come in, and we all queue like mad to get our share. Strike while the iron's hot, Mum says, but war or no war, they still taste yucky to me!

I asked Shirl about her night out with Alec, but she won't tell.

Friday, 30th August

Last night was very still and clear. As Dad went out for the evening shift, he looked up and said grimly, "If they're ever going to come, it'll be on a night like this."

And sure enough, the first air-raid warning came at a few minutes past nine. Mum was out at the ARP post, and Shirl, Tom and I were huddled together in the shelter with Chamberlain. Because it was clear, it was chilly too, and we needed the blankets and coats we'd taken down the garden with us.

Shirl's teeth were chattering already. "Cor blimey!" she said. "What's it going to be like in the middle of winter? I've got no feeling in my toes at all."

I could see Tom about to open his mouth to say something clever when we heard the first explosion, and then two more following close on the first one. The sound was heavy and sharp at the same time. Chamberlain's ears were pricked. He gave a long growl, and started towards the door of the Anderson. I held him back.

"Gawd, what was that?" gasped Shirl.

Tom's face was white in the candlelight, his eyes big and scared.

"It's started," I found myself saying.

We'd heard the bombs drop before we picked up the rumbling sound of the aircraft, but they weren't overhead and I selfishly said thank you to God because they weren't coming any nearer. Then we heard our gun batteries open up, rattling bullets towards the bombers.

"How close are they?" asked Tom shakily.

"Miles away," said Shirl, recovering herself and trying to sound confident. But as soon as she spoke, as if to put her in her place, there were two more explosions, this time much nearer. Chamberlain barked loudly. Now we could hear the bells of the fire engines too, and more frantic gunfire.

Then the drone of the aircraft faded, and we held our breath wondering if the planes were going to come back and what would happen if they did. But though the gun batteries kept chattering away, in a quarter of an hour or so the single long wail of the all-clear sounded, and we went inside to make ourselves a cup of tea and get warm.

"I hope Mum and Dad are all right," I croaked.

Shirl drummed her fingers on the kitchen table and looked at me. "Yeah. I hope so too," she said.

Saturday, 31st August

Dad told us at tea-time that the bombs had landed by a housing estate over near Downham. That really is miles away! The Lewisham Station had been called down there, but there was nothing to do. No one hurt, he said, and just a few big holes in the playing fields. Hitler'll have to do better than that, he laughed. But I could see he was putting a brave face on it for Mum, and she was wondering if she'd done the right thing taking on a job, and leaving us to cope.

"It's all right, Mum," I said, and I put my hand on hers across the table.

Wednesday, 4th September

One of the good things about my paper rounds is that if I get a quiet moment in the shop I can sneak a quick look at all the papers and magazines we don't get at home. I have to be careful not to put any creases or tears in them, mind, or I'd catch an earful from Mr Lineham.

Anyway, I can't remember where I read it, but apparently it's awful in the public shelters because of all the snoring. Stands to reason, I suppose.

In our family, Mum whistles a bit through her false teeth and Shirl makes a sort of piggy snorting sound. It's her adenoids, Mum says. But Dad takes the biscuit. He sounds like the band of the Royal Marines all on his own. So there's not much chance of sleep in *our* dugout, if we're all at home.

Can you imagine what it'd be like in an underground station full of people you didn't know, and trying to get some sleep? And if you wanted to go to the toilet, having to nip behind some piece of canvas on the platform and go in a bucket? Well, there's hundreds doing it every night. As Mum says, there's always someone worse off than yourself.

Sunday, 8th September

I'm trying to write this in the Anderson. There isn't much light and I'm all scrunched up in a corner so who knows whether I'll be able to make sense of it later on. It's half past six in the evening, but we've been here an hour or so already.

I feel small and scared, and dog-tired. None of us got much sleep last night. In fact, I think yesterday was the worst day of my life.

Everything was fine until the afternoon. The weather's been brilliant the whole of last week – not too hot, but clear and fresh. Dad had been given a day's leave so he went off, whistling a happy tune, to play cricket with his mates at Crofton Park. He doesn't get much chance these days.

In the morning, Mum had organized some games for the little kids over at the Hengist Road school, so I went along to give her a hand. Then Tom and me went down the market in the afternoon. Even if you don't buy anything, it's fun to listen to the traders. Each one's got his own patter, just like the comedians you get at the Hippodrome. One of them tells jokes about his mother-in-law all day long. The more you listen, the funnier it gets. Sometimes there's 50 standing around, laughing their heads off. Mind you, I wouldn't trust any of the stall-holders further than I could throw 'em.

It took everyone completely by surprise when the siren went. It must have been just after half past four.

There've been so many false alarms, people were getting fed up with it, so all you could hear was a sort of annoyed muttering in the crowd and among the traders. Of course, there's always some people who panic and rush for cover

44

straight away, but this time because it was so close to the end of the afternoon and the weather was so nice, most people were reluctant to pack up and go home.

I'd just said to Tom, "Come on then. We'd better go. . ." when a couple of people pointed up into the eastern sky over Eltham.

Glinting in the sun was a V-formation of silver crosses. There must have been twenty planes flying steadily over London.

"Where's the blinking RAF when you need them?" shouted someone.

People were running for cover now, and the market traders began to shove plates and pans into boxes and suitcases, then ripping the metal poles of the stands apart and throwing them on to the ground with a clatter.

We ran all the way back to Summerfield Road, and even before we reached number 47, we could faintly hear the distant sound of the first explosions. Mum was waiting at the door to scold us down the garden and into the Anderson, where for the next hour and a half we worried about Dad and Shirley.

At half past six, the all-clear sounded and we crawled outside, rubbing our eyes against the light.

Across the gardens beside the railway, the land lies fairly flat to the River Thames between Blackheath on one side and Lewisham Hill on the other. Rising into the sky from the direction of the river was a huge tower of evil, sinister, billowing smoke, slowly rolling over on itself, black at the bottom and turning grey at its height.

"Oh my word," Mum exclaimed. "It's the docks! Must be." And then, as if personally he could have done something about the massive fire, she said crossly, "Wherever's your dad got to? Blow the blooming cricket. . ."

In fact, as we trooped into the house one way, he was coming in at the front door, red-faced and breathing heavily, throwing off his cricket whites as he came.

"Better . . . go into . . . work. . ." he said between gulps of air. "They're going to need . . . all hands . . . on deck."

But even before he'd got out of the front door, the siren was screaming at us again and, carrying books, crossword puzzles, toys and blankets, we scurried back down to the Anderson.

We were there until *five o'clock in the morning*, more or less, and not a moment's sleep. There was a break in the middle of the evening just after it had got dark. Shirl had joined us by then, having scampered out of the public shelter down by Chiesman's.

"It don't half pong in there," she said, shaking the smell out of her hair, her nose shrivelling up in disgust. "I don't think half of Lewisham ever has a wash." She drew in a sharp breath. "Would you just look at that!"

We were standing in the garden, looking towards the river

again. The evening was still now, and though we could hear the occasional car and the bells of fire engines ringing their way across to Deptford, it was quiet enough to hear an animal rustle through the bushes on the railway embankment to our left. You get foxes up there sometimes.

But now where the smoke had been, the whole sky was an angry wound of red. We might be three or four miles away from the flames but with the amount of light they were making I could have easily read the paper Mum held.

"It's like the end of the world," Mum said slowly.

"Poor beggars," said Shirl.

"Is Dad over there?" asked Tom in a small voice.

"Him and every fireman in London, I shouldn't wonder," Mum answered, giving Tom a reassuring cuddle. "But then the whole city might be up in flames, for all we know. What a waste!"

Later in the evening, when Mum had gone off on duty, we could hear the drone of planes overhead more or less all the time. It's horrible. You feel the butterflies building up in your stomach till it almost becomes painful. I could see Shirl's fingers. The nails were bitten back hard, and her two hands were gripped together, the fingers sliding backwards and forwards over each other. It was about three o'clock when a stick of three bombs dropped closer than we'd ever heard before. They came through the air with a sound like the tearing of a curtain, and the explosions shook the ground. Chamberlain was beside himself with fear, past barking now, just trembling uncontrollably and whining pitifully.

We were all still white and shaking at breakfast. Mum wouldn't talk about the previous night. She fidgeted about the house, making a stew, dusting things that didn't need dusting, worrying about Dad.

Outside it was weird. If you looked down the street one way, it was a normal sunny Sunday morning, except everyone was more talkative than usual, leaning over fences and gates. Just over the road I could see Mrs Maclennan and Mrs Nott chatting to each other like they were old friends. This was strange, because everyone knew they hadn't got on for years. If you glanced the other way the pall of smoke hanging over the river reminded you of the nightmare you'd just been through.

Dad arrived home at noon, exhausted. He shook his head in despair. "I ain't ever seen anything remotely like it, Beattie," he said clasping a cup of tea in his hands. "It's a regular blinking inferno. All that oil, you see. I don't think we'll ever put it out."

Thursday, 12th September

It's the same every night now. Bombs and more bombs, and they're getting closer. A house got hit in Sandringham Road last night. That's one over from Summerfield. Sometimes I feel frightened and sometimes it makes me angry. The Germans don't seem to care who they might kill. What's going through the minds of the pilots when they drop their bombs? Haven't they got wives and families? So how can they try to kill other people's children?

I mean, I understand why they might want to bomb a factory that's making guns. I can even understand why they might try to hit a power station. But what difference does it make to the war if they kill Mum, or Tom? Or me?

Eventually they *did* put out most of the fire in the docks, despite what Dad said, but it took them a few days. According to Dad, it pretty much had to burn itself out.

Life's gone a bit funny. Sort of upside down. The best time to sleep is in the early morning, and because Mum and Dad both have to be out quite often at night, they try to catch a bit of kip during the daytime. So I seem to end up doing even more dishes and tidying up than normal. *And* most of the shopping too! Even Tom lends a hand from time to time. Mum says it's our bit towards the war effort, and put that way we can't grumble, can we?

Monday, 16th September

Mum came in on Friday night looking shaken up, eyes red as if she'd been crying. They'd been a bit short of wardens over at New Cross so she'd cycled up there to help out. There'd been a raid in the early evening, and a row of terraced houses had been hit – blasted to bits, Mum said.

"Sit down, Mum. I'll make you a cup of something," I said helplessly. As she took the cup of tea, her hands had a life of their own. They couldn't keep still.

"I think I'm a bit shocked, that's all love," she said. "Thanks for the tea, though. You're a good girl." And she burst into tears.

I just sat and watched. Mum wasn't *ever* like this. She got cross, but she never cried. When they went to the pictures together, it was the family's standing joke that Dad was more likely to cry than Mum.

After a minute or two she said, "I shouldn't be telling you, Edie, but I've got to talk to someone or I'll burst." She swallowed hard. "It was kids, you see. They were pulling kids out of the houses."

Now I understood. It was as if it could have been Tom or me.

"Poor things. I hope to God they never knew what hit them." She was crying again now. "We could hear a baby crying inside the rubble where a door had been. There was still a hole to get through but the blokes were too big. They said they couldn't ask me, but I knew what they wanted. I squeezed in all right, but she died in my arms. Poor little mite."

"Oh, Mum," I said and cuddled her. I didn't know what else to do. After a while she came to and asked, "Where's Tom?"

"I don't know," I said. He went out to play with Jim Simmonds about an hour ago.

Mum went spare. "*Why* don't you know?" she shouted. "What do you think you're here for? You're old enough to take some responsibility. You can't just let him wander off on his own. Anyone would think you were born stupid. Go and find him. And if he's not back in a quarter of an hour you'll both have your dad to answer to."

I didn't argue. Mum and I both knew what was going on. She'd been through a lot that day and she was taking some of it out on me, and that was all right this once. Tom was in the alley where I thought he'd be, kicking a ball around with

Jim. He looked a bit surprised to see me, though – almost guilty – and Jim stuffed something deeper into his pocket so I couldn't see.

Something's going on between those two. Jim isn't a good influence on Tom.

Thursday, 19th September

Mum's been pretty quiet since the weekend, not saying a word more than she has to. But then the lack of sleep's getting us all down, lying in the shelter each night wondering whether it'll be "our turn". That's the way people are starting to talk, like it's inevitable we'll all catch it in the long run.

Dad's trying to keep us all cheerful, but you can see in his eyes he's just so tired from working shift after shift. He's always kept himself fit and strong, but now he's so stiff and sore from all the work, he can scarcely lever himself out of his chair in the mornings.

In his time Dad must have seen some awful things. I shouldn't think you can avoid it if your job's putting out fires. He's never talked about it, and I shouldn't think he's going to now, but I wonder how much more even he can take.

Shirl isn't helping. She got in well after midnight on Wednesday evening. A party with friends from Chiesman's, she said. One *particular* friend, I reckon. It's that Alec, isn't it?

Dad gave her what for the next morning and told her not to do that again while she was living under his roof.

Shirl was very off-hand. "We might all be dead tomorrow," she said. "Eat, drink and be merry, I say. What's the problem as long as no one gets hurt?"

"There's lots of ways of getting hurt, girl," Dad said abruptly. "You're old enough to know that."

Saturday, 21st September

Right from the word go Mum was different this morning. She was back to her old self, brisk and organizing, as if this was a bright shiny new day, rather than the wet and windy one we'd actually got.

"Life must go on," she said. "It's what Hitler's after, isn't it – to have us moping around and thinking we can't cope. We've got to cope! 'Don't let the beggars grind you down.' That's my motto for the week."

And she took herself and the Mansion House polish outside to do the front step in the drizzle. Shirl, who has a late start at Chiesman's most Saturdays, raised a pencilled eyebrow at me.

There was a letter on the mantelpiece, tucked behind Mum's favourite china dog.

Shirl flicked it with a fingernail as she passed. "It's from Uncle Fred," she muttered. "Not good news, I shouldn't think."

But if it isn't, how come Mum's pulled herself together?

Tuesday, 24th September

Today Mum got me organized helping serve lunch down at the church hall to people who've been bombed out. The WVS (that stands for Women's Voluntary Service, in case you didn't know) are in charge, and don't they let you know it! They're a right bunch of old battle-axes, but I suppose their hearts are in the right place.

A lot of the people there have only got left what they're stood up in. No more house, no more furniture, no more clothes. Everything smashed and burnt. You'd think they'd be miserable, but they were yakking away over their dumplings like nobody's business. They get bread and jam in the mornings and evenings and a hot meal at midday. All free. When they've finished eating in the evenings, they stretch out on camp beds to try and get some sleep in between the raids.

In a spare moment, I sidled up to Mum and asked her about the letter on the mantelpiece. Her face fell for just a moment, and then she said quickly, "Shirl saw me open it, didn't she? Doesn't miss anything, that girl." She paused. "I won't kid you, Edie. It *is* bad news. Your Auntie Mavis died last Thursday. She went very quickly in the end. "

"That's very sad," I gulped. "Are *you* all right?"

"I knew it was coming," Mum answered. "I'd pushed it to the back of my mind, what with everything else. Then when the letter came I thought, Well we've got to get on with things while we can, haven't we? It made me cheer up, in a funny sort of way. Do you understand?"

I told her I thought I did.

Thursday, 26th September

When Shirl arrived for work at Chiesman's yesterday morning, she found one corner of the store missing, blown away the previous night by a bomb. All the windows were out and there was broken glass where you wouldn't think glass could get. Chiesman's weren't going to sell any china today or any ladies' hats and shoes, because they didn't have any, at least not in one piece.

"What did you do?" we asked Shirl.

"It's like you said, Mum. Don't let the beggars grind you down," she grinned. "We cleaned up the best we could. They told us the building wouldn't come down round our ears, but we shouldn't let the customers in yet. So while the chippies put up wooden partitions, me and the other girls carried some tables on to the pavement. Then we wrote a big sign saying, '*CHIESMAN'S: EVEN MORE OPEN THAN USUAL.*' It got a few laughs, I can tell you! And we took a few quid, too!"

We laughed along with Shirl, but it's not so funny when you think about it.

Tuesday, 1st October

It was Auntie Mavis's funeral yesterday, but only Mum made the trip down to Tonbridge. I wanted to go too, but Mum said with Dad working someone had to look after Tom. So that was me, wasn't it!

There'd been a heavy raid on Sunday night. The big bombs are bad enough, but the incendiaries are almost worse. They look like thin tin cans about eighteen inches long and they don't cause damage simply by blowing up, although I shouldn't think it'd do you much good if one landed on you from 10,000 feet. They just start fires everywhere, and the Fire Service can't keep up, Dad says. On bad nights, they don't know where to start. The Germans drop hundreds at a time.

There are delayed-action bombs too. They're really nasty, because they cause a mess when they land and then when people come to inspect the damage, the bomb goes off properly, taking anybody close-by with it. Every time Mum or Dad goes out I panic they're not going to come back.

When Mum had gone off to the station, looking sad and beautiful in her black dress, Tom hung around the house for a while, bored out of his skin, not helping with the cleaning. Then, about eleven o'clock, Jim Simmonds knocked on the door for Tom to go out and play. The two of them said they'd be up the alley as usual, pretending to be Charlton Athletic versus the Arsenal. I told Tom he should be back for lunchtime, and no messing about. If there was a siren, he was to come home at once.

Well, at 12.30 there wasn't a sign of them and after last time I started to worry.

Mum wasn't going to be back for hours, but if she ever knew Tom had been absent without leave she'd go off her rocker. At me as much as him!

I put Chamberlain on his lead and we walked up to the alley. It was empty.

"Tom, you little varmint," I said to myself. "Why am I always getting you out of trouble?"

They could have gone anywhere. I counted off Tom's favourite nooks and crannies in my head. The trouble was, the bombs were changing the geography of Lewisham every day. The Germans kept making new and exciting places for boys like Tom to be. It even interested me the way that if you dodged the officials you could see familiar things from different angles.

It was a risk either way. If Tom arrived at number 47 now, and found it deserted, *he* might panic. On the other hand I couldn't *not* search for them, could I?

I half-walked, half-ran down towards Catford Bridge, across the main road and along the edge of the slight hill on the far side. They weren't at the recreation ground, or behind the church. I cut through an alley where you could slip into the overgrown garden of a boarded-up house. There were trees there we all liked to climb. No Tom or Jim! It was one o'clock now and reluctantly I thought I'd better make for home.

We crossed the dirty old stream at the bottom of Mount Pleasant Road, where some sheds along the bank had been laid flat by a blast. Wood and rubble were strewn everywhere. From the far side, out of sight, I heard a shout that sounded suspiciously like Tom. Chamberlain's ears pricked and he woofed in the direction of the shout. I climbed down carefully and picked my way across. Everywhere smelled horrible. Drains, with a whiff of gas thrown in! The remains of a wall blocked my view. I pulled myself up on the crumbling bricks to see, and sure enough there were Tom and Jim. On the ground in front of them was a crumpled metal canister like a large tin-can. They looked like they might be about to use it as a football.

I bawled at the two boys, "Get away from that! Now! It might be a bomb, you stupid little blighters!"

Tom looked startled out of his wits, and the horrified look on my face must have convinced them. They backed off from the canister at a rate of knots.

I told Jim he could come back and have some chips and rice pudding with us, and that kept them quiet for half an hour or so, before they were running up and down the back garden path again, pretending to be Hurricanes and Spitfires shooting down German aircraft over Kent. I didn't let on to Mum about what had happened. It didn't seem fair.

Was it a bomb? I don't know, but I hope it taught my idiot little brother a lesson!

Yes, I know! Rice pudding! I'll make it, but I won't eat it.

Friday, 4th October

I don't know what's got into Tom. He was brought home by a policeman yesterday, of all things, and got a good hiding from Mum into the bargain. He and Jim and some other kids had been messing about on the running boards of what they thought was a disused van. Afterwards Tom said it was so covered with dust and dirt you couldn't see a thing through the windscreen. As if that made everything all right!

Well, the owner caught them, didn't he, and Tom was the one who couldn't run fast enough.

After she'd walloped him, Mum sent him upstairs and told him he couldn't go out for a week. She said she'd just about had enough of him running wild on the streets and she was getting to the end of her tether. She didn't want the neighbours thinking the Bensons were criminals. How dare he ruin the good name of the family!

I tried talking to him later up in his bedroom but he went all sulky on me, and in the end I gave up.

Last night Mum was still so upset she told the wardens she couldn't go in to work. She stayed in the Anderson with us, cuddling Tom through the raid and letting him know she loves him even though he is a complete donkey. We've made sleeping bags now, and with four of us in there it gets quite cosy. The one thing I like about it is the smell. It's a mixture of the paraffin lamp, and the grassy, damp earth.

Sometimes, in the odd moment when it's quiet – no guns, no bombs, no fire-bells, no planes – I can almost think we're having fun camping in the garden like we did before the war when I was a little girl. But the feeling never lasts long.

Saturday, 5th October

An awful thing happened near Lewisham station yesterday afternoon. A train was just rattling in from New Cross, and a German aircraft coming back from a raid over the river deliberately opened up its machine guns.

The pilot must have known exactly what he was doing. It's a miracle nobody in the train was killed. I hope his plane crashed on the way back to Germany. Or that Frank's boys shot him down. He doesn't deserve to live, if you ask me.

Shirl looked dreadful this morning. Huge circles under her eyes, and I couldn't get a peep out of her, no matter how much I tried to make her laugh. When she'd gone out I asked Mum if she knew what was wrong.

"It's that Alec fellow," she sighed. "Don't let on to Shirl I told you, but it turns out he's married. Never told Shirl of course, did he? Just been stringing her along these past couple of months. One of the other girls shopped him! I've a good mind to go into Chiesman's and tell him what I think of him, right there in the store!"

I didn't know whether she was serious or not, and she must have caught the look in my eye.

"No, well of course I won't!" she exploded. "But it'd make me feel better if I could. Why does Shirley always have to learn the hard way?"

Thursday, 10th October

They got the Hengist Road school last night, the one where Mum works. The wardens were all out looking after other people, thank goodness, so no one was hurt – but according to Mum it's a right mess. The building's three storeys high, with the hall on the ground floor and the classrooms on the two floors above, but now all the ceilings have gone and some of the walls are a bit dodgy, so Mum thinks it'll have to come down.

There've been raids every night now since September

7th. It's become a routine, like going to school or having breakfast. Sometimes it feels as if we're small furry animals, staying in our burrows during the night and popping out for a few hours during the day to eat and scavenge among the mess.

And the mess can be unbelievable. Imagine. A bomb lands on the pavement in front of a house. Even if it doesn't kill or injure anyone, it makes a huge hole in the road and scatters rubble and rubbish all over it, so the road's useless until it's cleared. All the windows of the house are blown out and maybe the front wall is unsafe, so the house may end up being pulled down. Of course the electric gets cut off and the water and gas mains may be broken, so everyone in the street ends up having to carry buckets up to stand-pipes at the end of the road just so they can clean their teeth. If you want to make tea, you'll have to do it on a primus stove!

And this happens a few times every day in Lewisham! And in most other parts of London too, from what Mum and Dad say.

Day by day, it's getting harder to have fun. The cinemas are closing down one by one. What's the point in staying open, if there's going to be an air-raid warning five minutes into the programme? We used to have sing-songs and games for the kids down at the school, but now that's history. There's still the wireless, of course, and we all listen in for programmes like *It's That Man Again*. Tuesdays at 9.30, bombs permitting. I think Tommy Handley is *so* funny. Mum tries to look disapproving and says I'm not old enough, but there's not much to laugh at in the world, is there? It's really strange how we all keep so cheerful.

Tuesday, 15th October

Tom's really gone and done it now. I thought he looked a bit sheepish when he came home for his tea last evening. Normally he bursts in, hair all over the place, making a noise, wanting something to eat, telling everyone what he's been doing, asking questions and telling daft jokes. Yesterday he sort of slunk in, and curled up in a corner looking at an old cartoon book he's had for years.

Later on we found out why. There was an unfriendly knock on the door and it was Mr Lineham from the corner shop, demanding to see Mr or Mrs Benson please. He didn't look very comfortable. His eye twitches a bit when there's something not right, and now it was going nineteen to the dozen. Mum was late to go out and already looking a bit harassed, but she dried her hands on the dishcloth she was holding and took Mr Lineham, still twitching, into the front parlour.

I was a bit scared. I thought *I* must have done something wrong. Maybe he'd come to complain about me being too slow delivering the papers, or putting them through the wrong doors. But it wasn't me he was after. It was Tom.

After a bit Mum came out of the front parlour very quietly and asked me, "Where's Tom? I want him."

She was so calm, I knew something was up.

But Tom wasn't there. He must have slipped out of the back door when he'd seen Mr Lineham arrive.

"Go and find him," Mum said firmly. "We've given that boy enough chances. We've got to put a stop to this once and for all!"

So off I went again, trailing the streets after Tom in the drizzle, this time knowing it was about to get dark, and there might be a siren any minute.

You remember that back garden I told you about, the one that's all overgrown? Well, I reckoned that's where he'd be. We'd made a sort of camp there last spring, and he'd know it would at least keep him dry for an hour or so. When I found him huddled under the dripping trees, he looked small, frightened and pathetic. He cowered away from me, shaking so much the words wouldn't come out properly.

"What's ... going ... to ... happen?" he sobbed. "I don't ... want ... to go ... to prison."

I wasn't going to let him off the hook yet. I didn't know what he'd done at that point, but it obviously wasn't very clever. "Well, you should have thought of that sooner," I said, hauling him to his feet. "What on earth have you been up to?"

"It . . . was . . . Jim's idea," he wailed.

"Oh yes," I said, "and whatever it was, you had no part in it I suppose?"

I expected Mum to go up the wall when we got back to number 47, but she stayed very calm. She took Tom into the parlour to apologize to Mr Lineham. I expect for a few minutes she also had visions of Tom languishing in a prison cell.

Eventually the parlour door opened and Mr Lineham stepped on to the street, raising his little black hat to Mum one last time and saying twitchily, "I'm sorry to have troubled you, Mrs Benson, but, ehmm, it's for the best in the long run. . ."

It turned out Tom and Jim had been in the shop yesterday afternoon. While Jim was buying some ha'penny chews, Tom had pocketed a couple of toy soldiers from the other end of the counter.

I could have told him old Lineham doesn't miss a trick. He's had that shop for years, and he knows enough to keep eyes in the back of his head when two small boys come in together.

Mum was her usual self the rest of the evening, apart from the fact she had to send Shirl down to give her apologies to the ARP again, but it's left me with an uncomfortable feeling in the stomach. I just know we haven't heard the last of this.

Friday, 18th October

So now I know the worst, and it's just about as bad as it could be. Mum took me on one side after breakfast this morning. Her face was lined with worry. She didn't look as if she'd slept a wink.

"Edie," she said, taking my hands in hers. "I've arranged for you and Tom to go away for a while. I know I said I never would, but this is no good, is it?"

I was shocked rigid. "No, Mum," I said. "You can't do it. Where would we go? Who would we stay with?" Although I desperately didn't want to, I started to cry, and then she joined in and for a few minutes I just held on to her, sobbing my guts out.

"It's not just that business with Tom and Mr Lineham, love," she said eventually, when we'd both calmed down a bit. "'Though I'm at my wits' end with him, really I am. It's not even as though you can say it's Tom's fault. This isn't proper living, is it? He needs a break, and so do you. I've been to see the authorities down at the Town Hall and they've found you a place in the country. South Wales, near Brecon. On a farm I think. It'll be safe there. I had to pull a few strings to get you out of Lewisham quick."

I knew there wasn't a hope of changing her mind, but I was appalled.

"How long for?" I croaked hopelessly.

Mum looked me straight in the eye. "You're a big girl now, Edie, so I'm going to treat you like one. I honestly can't say for how long. But there's people moving out of Lewisham every day now. You must have cottoned on to that. Who knows how long Hitler can keep throwing the kitchen-sink at us? There doesn't seem to be any sign of a let-up. And it worries me things might be much, much worse this winter."

"I don't want to leave you and Dad," I wept. "I couldn't bear it if anything happened."

"Your dad agrees with me," she said firmly. "Turn it on its head! How do you think we could live with ourselves if we kept you here and either of you got hurt? In the end Mrs Chambers was right, though I hate to admit it. You've got to go."

And the way she argues it, in the end I suppose I agree with her.

Monday, 21st October

When they told Tom, it was terrible. He just howled and howled for what seemed like hours. They must have heard it up the other end of the street. At about tea-time, I went out with him down to the one set of swings in Lewisham they haven't melted down for the war effort. I tried really hard to be as enthusiastic as I knew how. I told him what fun we were going to have.

"Just think," I said, "no more sleeping in a crummy old shelter. No more dodging the bombs."

"But what is there to do in Wales?" he said despondently.

"Don't know till we get there, do we?" I answered brightly.

I can see his point. And I bet I know the other thing that's worrying him. It worries me slightly too. School!

Sunday, 27th October

The air-raid warnings came late last night, so at least we got an hour or two in bed before we decamped to the shelter.

As we were turning in, Shirl fished around in her handbag and pulled out two large, white, five pound notes. She pushed them into my hand.

"For a rainy day," she said, with a shy grin. I was astonished. Ten pounds is a *lot* of money. I've never held so much in my hand at one time.

"What are you doing, Shirl?" I asked. "You can't afford this. It must have taken you weeks and weeks to save!"

"Look after it then," she said. "I'm not going to complain if you bring it back with you, am I? But, like I say, you might need it."

I hugged and hugged her. When it's mattered, Shirl's always been there for me.

Monday, 28th October

Our train was supposed to leave Paddington station in West London at eight this morning. Dad's boss – Mr Abbott – was a star and took us there in his Austin.

"You didn't need to do this, Reg," my dad said as Mr Abbott stood on the doorstep, stifling a yawn. Like Reg Abbott's, Dad's face was raw and red from working the previous night. There was a cut on his cheek and his right sleeve was rolled back to stop it rubbing on a painful burn that ran a good four or five inches up towards the elbow.

"'Course I did, Bert," said Mr Abbott. "At least you'll know the nippers have done one bit of the journey safely. Are you fit?"

We hugged Mum and Shirl tearfully and I smoothed Chamberlain's beautiful ears back one last time.

"Be good," said Mum pointedly to Tom, looking him

deep in the eyes. "Do what Edie tells you. I'll be thinking of you every other minute, I shouldn't wonder." And before she lost control, she bundled us into the back of the car with a final kiss. Only Shirl stayed on the pavement to wave us goodbye.

"Don't get too used to having the room to yourself," I shouted at her through the window. "We're not going to be that long."

She grinned. "I promise," she said. "What am I going to do with no one to moan at?"

The excitement of being in the car kept Tom's mind occupied. Somewhere near Vauxhall we had to steer our way cautiously round a tram that was leaning over crazily, its front half down a crater in the road.

Dad let out a low whistle as we drove past. "Nasty," he said. "I hope that wasn't as bad as it looked!"

It was a misty, damp morning. In one street you'd think there wasn't a war on at all. People were beginning to make their way smartly to work, carrying bags and newspapers. And in the next grey and mournful street, where a bomb had fallen or there'd been a recent fire, the inhabitants were either standing on their doorsteps looking dazed at the destruction around them or disconsolately setting to work with brooms and shovels to put a bit of order and normality back in their lives.

Under the curved metal roof of Paddington station where

the smoke from the locomotives hung greasily in the girders, we said our second lot of goodbyes.

Tom and I found ourselves seats, and pulled down the window in the compartment, squeezing our heads round the blackout blind.

"We're not going to hang around," Dad shouted. "Going home to get some shut-eye." And suddenly we were on our own.

When the little slow train from Cardiff at last pulled into Llantrisant station it was five o'clock, and even Tom had had enough of trains for one day. The platform was eerily quiet apart from the hissing of steam and the birds tweeting. Bushes hung over the fences looking badly in need of a haircut. We were the only passengers getting off, but as if there was any danger of missing us, a scowling man stood by the station building holding a piece of cardboard high in the air. On it was scrawled the one word: "BENSON". The writing was worse than Tom's. The man was overweight and bald. A pair of leather braces barely kept his stomach and his dirty trousers from falling apart.

"That's got to be Mr James," I said, pulling our battered old suitcase out of the carriage on to the gravelled platform.

"He doesn't look very pleased to see us," Tom muttered.

We must have looked odd, standing there with our gas masks around our necks in their cardboard boxes, and our old school satchels (full of the few home comforts we could bring with us) falling off our shoulders. Suddenly the gas masks seemed completely unnecessary. There was nothing to tell you there was a war on in Llantrisant. Even the station name stood out defiantly on the board beside us. The paint looked new.

"You've got here, then," was all Mr James could say in welcome, his voice a sing-song Welsh. "This way. You'd better hurry up or you'll miss tea." And leaving us to struggle with the luggage, he lumbered through the building to the drive outside the station where a tractor and a wagon were parked.

He jerked a thumb at the wagon where high up there were a couple of rough seats facing back up the road. "That's for you up there, see!" he said. "You can climb up," he went on, though it sounded more like an order than a request.

Tom was riveted to the spot. He just stood there gawping.

"Didn't you 'ear me?" said Mr James rudely. "In the wagon. Quick now."

Whether it was lack of food after a day's travelling or just the bucking and swaying of the cart, I don't know, but I felt sick after a few yards, so it was a good job the station and the small village of Llantrisant were only a couple of miles from the farmhouse. Throwing up all over Mr James's wagon wouldn't have got us off to a good start, would it?

Tuesday, 29th October

I've got to be positive, and I've got to be strong. I told myself before we left home that this was going to be hard. I just didn't know quite *how* hard. I'm missing Mum and Dad and number 47 like mad. There's a gnawing pain in my stomach, and I find I keep wanting to cry. Last night when we were all in bed, I couldn't help myself, and I really did weep buckets. I hope Tom didn't hear me. Most of all, I've got to be brave for his sake.

So, what are the good points of Llantrisant? Well, to start with, obviously we're safe. Not even the Jerries would think it was worthwhile bombing this place. There's nothing much here except us and the cows.

Then, except for the strange musty smell, I suppose the James's farmhouse is nice. We've got a room each and they're so big we're rattling around in them. Big and cold!

The furniture's a bit rickety, but it's not as though my clothes even a quarter-fill the drawers and wardrobe in the room. I put Freddie my mascot bear on the chest of drawers facing the bed so that I can always see him. He's been with me as long as I can remember. Then I arranged the five books

I've brought with me on the shelf. I took Shirl's money, and carefully slipped one five pound note inside the dust jacket of *Diary of a Nobody*, by George and Weedon Grossmith, and one inside the cover of *Winnie the Pooh*. I think the money should stay a secret between me and Shirl for now.

My bed's a bit odd. It's really high off the ground and the mattress sags badly at the sides, so it's rather like sleeping on top of a roof. I feel as if I'm going to fall off at any moment.

Looking out of the bedroom window this morning, I can see that the countryside's very pretty. The fields all around us are a bright, beautiful green, and in the distance I can see hazy, furry, flat-topped hills with shadows passing over the purple. They remind me of the cushions on the settee in the front parlour at home. But I mustn't think too much about that.

On the other hand, there's not much good to say about Mr and Mrs James. From the photographs on the mantelpiece in the dining room, Tom and I reckon they must have three grown-up children. If they treated them like they treated us last night, I should think the kids must have left home as soon as they could. Why did they take us in, if they hate us so much? During tea and then before we went to bed, Mr James scarcely said a word and if he did it was rude or cross. On the other hand, Mrs James never let up. She seemed to have it in for me more than Tom. "*Don't put your elbows on the table! Don't gobble your food! Don't scrape your chair on the floor!*" (The floor in the dining room's made of stone, and the chairs make a noise on it.) *"Don't talk with your mouth full!"* (When she'd just asked me a question!)

Then there were the personal comments about my hair (*scruffy!*) and my dress (*too short and too many patterns!*).

Thursday, 31st October

I couldn't face writing yesterday. It would have come out all miserable and depressed. Just like the weather.

Shirl said it rained a lot in Wales, and now I believe her. It started on Tuesday afternoon, and it's poured down more or less ever since.

To keep us from getting bored, the Dragon's had us working for our living. (Well, I'm right that the dragon's a Welsh national emblem, aren't I? It seems to suit Mrs James rather well.) She's had the two of us cleaning her silver and helping with the washing. It hasn't taken us long to find out that nothing's ever good enough.

But we had two letters from home today, one from Mum and Dad and the other from Shirl, and that made us feel better and worse all at the same time. I'm so mixed up, but underneath everything else, I really wish we could go home.

The food here's just about all right, but Tom can't cope

with the Dragon's soup, all watery cabbage. Yesterday he ended up having nothing but chewy bread and yucky jam for tea, because he couldn't finish his bowl of gruel! There's plenty of vegetables from the farm, so we won't be short of beetroot sandwiches, but boy, are we going to miss our fish and chips!

Saturday, 2nd November

Yesterday's chore was gathering kindling for the James's fire. The Dragon packed us off with baskets over the fields behind the farm to a small copse. And one journey wasn't enough. Oh no! She had us backwards and forwards at least five times. Now we've got enough wood to keep a fire going all winter, if we have to!

It was an easy enough job because the way the wind's been blowing up these last few days it's brought down loads of small branches and twigs from the trees. I don't mind having something to do. It's just the way she seems to think we're here for her personal convenience, like we're servants or something. There's never a please or thank you, it's simply "Do this!" or "Do that!" Or just as often: "*Don't* do that!"

In the afternoon, she sent us off to the stores in Llantrisant to buy some bread and tea. I've been carrying an emergency supply of coppers in the pocket of my skirt and I was feeling so down, I thought I'd try and phone Dad from the call box by the crossroads in the middle of the village.

I just wanted to hear a friendly voice, but when I got through to the fire station in Lewisham, Dad was out on a "shout", and all I could do was leave a message with the duty desk. This time I couldn't help it. When I'd put the phone down I cried my eyes out in sheer frustration as Tom looked on pathetically. It can't be nice to see your big sister properly upset. In the end he put a sticky hand on my arm and I came to.

"I'll be all right now," I sniffed. "Don't mind me. I shouldn't have done it. I shouldn't have phoned. It won't change anything, will it?"

Sunday, 3rd November

Today must rank as one of the most boring ever. It was a sort of Chapel sandwich. We had to walk to Chapel with Mr and Mrs James for the eleven o'clock morning service, then walk back to the farm for lunch, then back to Sunday School (at the Chapel) in the afternoon, and then (would you believe it?) there was another lot of Chapel in the evening! And the James's call Sunday a "day of rest"!

The Chapel is an angry red brick building in the middle of Llantrisant, with "BETHESDA 1888" carved into a large piece of stone high on the front. As you stand in the street it feels like the three big arched windows are like eyes following you as you go, and inside it felt pretty much the same. Everyone turned to look at us when we walked in. Did we each have two heads, I asked myself?

Morning and evening the Reverend Gwynfor Evans – he's the pastor at Bethesda – preached a sermon that must have lasted 45 minutes. In the evening I had to keep kicking Tom on the ankle so he wouldn't fall asleep. And scary stuff it was too, all about sin, hell-fire and damnation. The gist of it was that if we didn't do what we were told (and I'm sure he kept looking at Tom and me) we were going to burn for certain. Which, given that we've come to Wales to escape just that, seems a bit funny really.

But I tell you what, they can certainly sing round here. I've never heard anything like it. A hundred and fifty people in that chapel, and they were making more noise than the crowd do down at The Valley when Charlton are playing at home.

Sunday school was just awful. The other kids gawped at us, and in between singing and praying we had to kneel on the grubby floor of the chapel hall and use our chairs as a sort of table to colour in some silly pictures of Moses in the bulrushes. I ask you, how old do they think we are? Tom gave up in disgust, so I expect we're both marked down as members of the awkward squad now.

Monday, 4th November

Today we went to a real school for the first time in a year. Well, at least it's something to do, and gets us away from the smell of the pigs. There's only the one class in the village school and Miss Williams the teacher seems sweet. She's quite young and friendly, with beautiful long brown hair done in ringlets. I think she feels sorry for us. In the afternoon, she made us tell the rest of the children about life in Lewisham. You should have seen their eyes when we told them about the bombing. They were standing out on stalks.

I'm one of the oldest, so I don't think they'll give me any bother, but I'll have to look out for Tom. There's one ginger kid who might be trouble.

Tuesday, 5th November

Firework night! But there won't be any fireworks in Llantrisant this evening. I don't think the Welsh would have cared if

Guy Fawkes had got away with blowing up the Houses of Parliament. London seems a very long way away.

And thinking of Mum and Dad and dear Shirl (and Frank and Maureen too), I hope there aren't too many fireworks over their way either!

School's difficult, though the work's really easy-peasy. But I know I can't keep putting my hand up to answer questions or I'll look a right little show-off.

And every time my back's turned, I catch that ginger kid giving Tom the eye. His name's Philip Morgan, and he's obviously used to being cock of the walk round here. Two things I don't understand about boys. One is why they're dirty so much of the time. The other is why they're always fighting.

Wednesday, 6th November

A bad day. The Dragon's getting worse. She picks me up on everything I do. According to her I'm the most impolite, selfish person there's ever been. I'm trying really hard, and all she can do is tell me how dreadful I am.

And then there's Tom. I thought he was beginning to cope. He's smiled a bit more in the last day or so, but then I turned my back on him for no more than five minutes at lunchtime, and suddenly there he was, hunched up in a corner with a bloody nose. You've guessed it. Philip Morgan!

Tom's never been bullied in his life, so I asked him, "Why did you let him do it? I hope you gave him a fourpenny one in return!"

Tom shook his head miserably.

"Why not?" I said in amazement.

"He said they'd all come and get me," he snivelled.

Well I saw red, didn't I? I wasn't having my little brother being pushed around. "We'll see about that," I said, and before school started again after lunch I collared the Morgan kid and shoved him up against a wall. He was very surprised. I don't think a girl had ever spoken to him like that before.

"Look," I said, "do that again, and you'll need a hospital. Understand?" I hope he didn't see me shaking, as he crept away to find a stone to hide under. And there's me complaining about *boys* fighting all the time. Well isn't the message of the war that we have to stand up to bullies?

Anyway, then he went and told on me to "nice" Miss Williams, who turned into not-so-nice Miss Williams. And somehow by the end of the afternoon word had got back to the Dragon her London kids were ruffians and thugs and that it wouldn't do.

So neither of us had anything to eat tonight, and Tom's beside himself with homesickness and anger. I tiptoed out of my room into his to try and hold him together.

"Stick it out," I whispered. "It'll get better, you'll see!"

"It won't," he moaned, miserably. "I want to go home. I hate this place and I hate school. I want my mum. I've had enough!"

"Tom," I said, starting to wonder if he might do something stupid, "listen to me. Give it a week. If it isn't better by then, we might have to think again. But give it a week. Trust me. All right?"

In the end, he nodded his head.

Thursday, 7th November

We had a letter from Mum today, but I had to more or less prise it out of the Dragon's grasp.

If she hadn't dropped the pile of newspapers she was carrying, I don't think we'd ever have seen it. She looked really annoyed as the letter fluttered from between the newsprint down on to the floor and I helpfully picked it up for her, but she covered her tracks quickly.

"I was just going to give you that," she said without a hint of a blush. "Is it from your mum and dad?" As if it was from anyone else!

Still, they all seem fine, and say not to worry about

anything. No mention of my telephone call. Perhaps the message was never passed on?

Friday, 8th November

Things are going from bad to worse. Now Tom's ill!

He said he didn't feel too clever on Thursday evening, but then he woke me in the middle of the night to tell me in a very small weak voice that he'd been sick all over his bed. Only the sheets actually, so that wasn't too bad.

I tiptoed around trying not to wake anyone, cleaning poor Tom up, pulling the soiled sheets off his bed and replacing them with mine, and finding him a glass of water and a bowl so that if he was sick again the same thing wouldn't happen. Finally I found an extra moth-eaten blanket in the cupboard and wrapped it around myself till the morning.

In the morning I got to the Dragon as early as I could. I knew she'd give someone a rollicking, and I wanted it to be me, not Tom. She raged and banged around for a bit, saying that she didn't have the time to be bothered with stupid children, but in the end she gave me some spare sheets with the threat that they'd have to stay on "for a fortnight at least".

Sunday, 10th November

Tom's still not completely better. He's up and about now, but he's still complaining of a dreadful headache, and it's obvious he's got absolutely no energy. I don't think he'll make it to school tomorrow. Still, at least we got out of Chapel and Sunday School – Tom because he was ill, and me because I had to look after him, didn't I?

Before the Dragons came home in the evening I took my chance and used their tin bath in front of the living room fire for half an hour, boiling up half a dozen kettles on the stove to get the water hot enough.

I got everything put away in the nick of time before they came in. But it's very hard not to leave any wet marks behind when you're trying to wash yourself in a tin bath, and I prayed they wouldn't see the damp patch I'd left on the rug.

Monday, 11th November

The Dragon more or less forced Tom to go to school this morning, accusing him of being a malingerer. I had to explain to Tom she wasn't saying he'd got a dreadful disease, just that he was lazy! The poor boy sat and shivered by the stove in the schoolroom all day, and even Miss Williams and the other children could see he wasn't up to working and left him alone.

In the evening the Dragon came up to my room to call me for dinner, and sort of hung about as if she was trying to find the words to say something important to me. Maybe she'd decided she actually wanted a conversation after two weeks of shouting. I'd been reading my *Jane Eyre* and she eyed my little row of books suspiciously, up and down, up and down. For a moment I was afraid she was going to tell me reading was a waste of time (which was obviously what she was thinking) and confiscate the books and their hidden hoard of treasure. But she contented herself with a tetchy shake of the head, as if she pitied me, and turned on her heels.

Wednesday, 13th November

I've never done anything really bad in my life before, but I think I might be about to, and I feel all tied up in knots about it.

When I think about it, even in the mornings when I'm at my most cheerful, the last fortnight's been horrible. After that bother with Philip Morgan, the other kids at school have just ignored us. I'd say they've sent us to Coventry, but since we're in Wales that doesn't seem quite right, does it? Maybe they've sent us to Cardiff then! (You can see I haven't completely lost my sense of humour!)

After the first day or so, we just stopped bothering about it, talked to each other, and got on with what Miss Williams gave us to do. She's gone all stand-offish too, but perhaps that's just in my imagination. That's the trouble, you see: keeping things in proportion.

The final straw came today. It's a week since I said to Tom I was sure things would improve, and I was wondering what I was going to say to him after school today because I knew they hadn't. Anyway, that's when it happened. I wasn't there, mind. I only saw the results.

For the last couple of days now, Mr and Mrs Dragon have been pushing Tom outside to help with small things on the farm, even though he's not really better – pulling up vegetables for supper, piling silage on to the wagon, watching how the cows are milked and so on. That's all right, I suppose. The fresh air's probably good for him, and it's better than him hanging round the house getting bullied along with me.

Anyway, Mr James had Tom in his workshop this afternoon, supposedly teaching him some woodwork. Tom told me he'd been practising knocking nails into a bit of wood with one of Mr James's hammers when he missed the nail and hit his thumb hard.

I don't know what Tom said because he won't tell me, and I can't think it can have been too awful, because I don't think he knows many really bad words, but whatever it was shocked old James. I don't think Chapel folk swear very much, though it doesn't prevent them being as rude as they like.

So Mr James comes back in the house literally holding Tom by the ear, and tells the Dragon what he's said. Now once or twice I've heard Mum use the expression "*Wash your mouth out with soap and water*" when someone's said a rude word, but I never dreamed anyone would really do it. But that's exactly what they did. Mr James held Tom down, and she applied the soap. None too gently either.

I was shocked. As Tom began to howl I started to say they

should leave him alone, but the Dragon roughly told me to be quiet or I'd be next for the high jump.

When they'd finished it was the usual thing. Tom was sent upstairs and told not to come down till he was called. I went with him and dared them to stop me.

Anyway, I've made my mind up. We can't stay here. Not after that! We've given it our best shot, and things aren't going to get any better.

Thursday, 14th November

I've thought about this very carefully, and we're not going to get two chances. We've got to make our escape work first time.

Thank heavens for the money Shirl gave me. If ever there was a "rainy day" this has got to be it!

After school today, Tom and I went to spy out the land at Llantrisant station. The timetable on the platform says there's just two trains a day to Cardiff, but the good news is one of them's at 8.25.

If we say we're going down to school ten minutes early tomorrow morning we can be on that train. Most of our luggage will have to stay here: all we can carry is our school bags.

I said a special prayer tonight for the train not to be cancelled. What'll happen when we get home I've got no idea, but the only way to convince Mum and Dad about this is face to face. A letter won't do.

Friday, 15th November

The man in the ticket office peered over his glasses very suspiciously when we bought two singles for Paddington. It was exactly 8.22 and down the platform the little tank engine was already champing at the bit in front of the three carriages that made up the 8.25 for Cardiff.

We had the money, didn't we? I looked him straight in the eye when I handed it over, as if this was what we did every day of the week.

He stared right back, knowing he'd seen us before, but not quite able to make the right connection. I held my breath and waited for him to say something, but then he dropped his gaze and slowly, oh so slowly, gave me the change. This time there were some other passengers on the train so he couldn't keep them waiting just because we looked a bit dodgy, could he?

All the way to Cardiff I think we both expected the train

to creak to a halt any minute, and a copper to come and haul us off. But it rumbled on into the grey stone suburbs, and just after ten we were standing scanning the destination board inside the station canopy.

There was an express for Paddington at 10.45. If we made that, we were safe. Once in London, even if by chance they rounded us up, I reasoned they'd have to take us home and not back to Llantrisant.

Every time a ticket collector banged his way down the corridor on the express, every time the door of our compartment slid back, every time someone in uniform passed down the train, I thought the game was up. Now I know what it must feel like to be a spy behind enemy lines.

Whenever the train pulled up at a signal, our hearts began to beat faster. At Swindon, wherever that is, it stopped for a full fifteen minutes though it wasn't meant to, and I thought we'd had it. But no one came, and eventually the train wheezed back into life.

Every chance I got I talked quietly to Tom, encouraging him, telling him why we were doing what we were doing and how well we were getting on. He was as scared as I was. *I* knew he didn't normally look that pale and wan, but nobody else did so that was all right. As the day went on, hunger made us even more edgy, but I didn't want to spend any of our precious cash till we were safely in London. Food could wait. We weren't going to die of starvation.

Finally, after hours of sitting on the edge of our seats, the train drew slowly into Paddington. As we handed our tickets in at the barrier I felt like doing a dance, but of course the worst bit was still to come. Facing the music at number 47!

Tom must have been reading my mind.

"Food?" I said. "Or home first?"

"Home," he said decisively.

Saturday, 16th November

I was dog tired last night, and almost fell asleep over the diary. And there was a miracle! No air-raid sirens. No bombs! I slept through till nine in the morning, and I don't remember a thing.

Now where was I in the story?

Well, we caught the tube to Charing Cross, and then the Southern Electric to Lewisham. It was easier than working out which buses were running. I haven't been in the tube for months. The Circle line runs only just underground, not like the Northern where you have to go down hundreds of stairs, so it isn't great as a shelter. Even so, tonnes of people move in every night from the look of things. They're supposed to clean up every morning, but there's still lots of stuff left around. And the disgusting smell hits you in the face the minute you walk inside. I don't know how the people who camp out there don't catch dreadful diseases.

When we walked in the back door of number 47, Mum was doing the washing. When she saw us her face was a picture. In an instant the colour bleached out of her, and I thought she was going to faint. She caught hold of the mangle for support, and then without a word the three of us hugged till we cried.

She knew. Just from the fact we were there, she knew. "You're a truthful girl, Edie," she said later in the evening, when I'd stopped explaining. "I know you wouldn't have done it unless you had to." Finally, she relaxed and leaned back slightly in her chair. Pursing her lips in a half-smile, she said, "So what are we going to say to Mr and Mrs Dragon, then?"

Tom had been subdued and serious all through the evening, but as he caught the twinkle in Mum's eye, he laughed and laughed with relief until his sides ached. I'd forgotten the smell of home, of cosiness and baking and polish, and now I want to stay here for ever.

As I was falling asleep last night, Shirl came and put her arms around me and planted a kiss on my forehead "Good on you, girl," she said. "I hope I'd have done exactly the same."

Tuesday, 19th November

We came back at the right time. Jerry's leaving London alone now, but from what I read in the paper yesterday, that means other people are having it even worse than we did. Last weekend they say Coventry was badly hit, and pretty well burned to a cinder. And today they've sent all the Lewisham regular firemen and a lot of the auxiliaries up to Birmingham. The fires there are burning right out of control. Who knows when Dad'll be home!

Mum says perhaps Hitler's seeing sense. He thought he could bomb the spirit out of the British people, but now he knows he can't. It makes me feel sort of proud. Back in September, when the RAF won the "Battle of Britain" by seeing off the German bombers, Mr Churchill said never had so much been owed by so many to so few, and I thought of how our Frank was one of those few. Well someone has to keep the planes flying, don't they! Not everyone can get the glory of shooting down Messerschmitts.

And now we've all done our bit by not giving in. Maybe even Tom and me, by not staying in Wales.

The fact the bombing's stopped made it easier for Mum

and Dad not to send us back to the Dragons, though we've had some old-fashioned looks from a few people who knew we'd gone. Mr Lineham, for one. He didn't mind having me back to help with the papers, though. (By the way, newspapers are shrinking every week. The government wants all the paper it can lay its hands on for the war effort.)

On the other hand, I've heard they're opening the elementary schools again next month. I'm too old now, but Tom'll have to go. I think Mum's relieved. Now at least she'll know where Tom is every day.

Wednesday, 20th November

Dad's still in Birmingham and there's been no news. I'm not used to Dad being away, and when I think about it the hairs on the back of my neck go all hot with worry.

One of the main reasons I'm glad to be back at number 47 is the food. I didn't realize till I went away how good a cook Mum is, and Shirl too come to that.

What with the shortages and the rationing, it's getting harder to make do, but Mum says that's where a good cook can really shine. Bacon's rationed, and so is butter and margarine of course, and now tea. I suppose that's obvious since it comes to England in ships, and the German U-boats are blowing up so many of them. There's not much chance of proper meat anymore, so we have to put up with liver and kidneys. And ox tongue. Actually, I'm starting to really like that. Tinned salmon's nice, too. We eat a lot more veg than we used to, and Mum makes us keep up our vitamins by drinking tomato juice, which I can't say I like. It's far too slimy!

We can still get fresh eggs, but Mum reckons we'll be lucky if they're not rationed too before long. She wants us to keep chickens, so at least we'll have the eggs from them.

It's Mum's puddings I like best: jam roly-poly and honey-and-walnut cake are my favourites. If *I* try to make them they just aren't the same.

The queues at shops are getting longer now that people are starting to think about Christmas, so I expect I'll be doing a lot of hanging around in the cold. Everyone tries it on to get more than their fair share. When the war started you heard some dreadful stories about rich people turning up in their chauffeur-driven cars and cleaning out shops far away from where they lived. That's why rationing was brought in, and why we can only get rationed goods from the shop where we're registered – in our case, Nuttall's for the meat, and Harrold's for the groceries.

You can't always trust shopkeepers either. They might

seem as nice as pie, but a bloke in Deptford was had up for watering down his milk the other day and selling eggs that were smaller than they were supposed to be.

Of course, if you're in with the shopkeepers there's always the chance you can get something "under the counter", on the black market. It's funny how some people always seem to have cigarettes, and other people can't get them for love nor money. Not that I want them, only Shirl!

Saturday, 23rd November

It's rained cats and dogs for the last 24 hours, and the River Ravensbourne's flooded. Half a mile away there's mud and rubbish all over people's houses, as if things haven't been bad enough.

Dad's back from the Midlands, and I've never seen him like this. Even when the Blitz here was at its worst, he usually came up smiling, but this is different. He came home and went to bed without saying a word. He must have slept twelve hours solid.

97

Sunday, 24th November

It was just Dad and me this morning. He'd been tidying up the garden and I caught him when he was putting his tools away in the garden shed. I asked him what was wrong.

"It was awful, love," he answered in a low voice. "I've seen some things, but this was like nothing else. . ." And his voice trailed off into nothing. I could see he was close to tears. He pulled himself together, and this time when he spoke it was with anger, even hatred.

"They hit a school where there were kids having a party," he said eventually. "There were maybe 40 inside. We got there too late. It was just one great wall of flame. Choking fumes and smoke everywhere. We tried our best to get in, time after time, but it was no good. Do you know what they say it was, Edie? An oil bomb! I ask you, what kind of perverted minds drop bombs that spray burning oil on five-year-old kids? And I couldn't do a damn thing to help." He was openly crying now with the memory of the horrors he'd seen. I went and put my arms round him, but there was nothing I could do. There were terrifying pictures in his mind and nothing I said would ever wipe them out.

Tuesday, 26th November

With winter coming on, everyone's talking about getting ill. What's worrying is all those folk crowded together in the big public shelters. The bombs may have stopped for a bit, but everyone's sure Hitler'll come back to London one day soon, and most people don't want to take a chance. It's cold and dirty in the tube stations. People even go down to the caves in Chislehurst every night, because they think they'll be safe. But what if there's an epidemic of flu? Apparently, in 1918, it killed tens of thousands of people just after the Great War, and maybe the same thing will happen again this time. Except it might be diphtheria, or the plague. It just doesn't bear thinking about. With all those people coughing over each other, any illness could spread like wildfire.

I've started cycling over to help out at a Red Cross centre for bombed-out people in Deptford, and that's opened my eyes I can tell you!

At night there's only buckets for toilets, and not even enough of those. I won't go into it too closely, but sometimes in the morning there's stuff leaking all over the floor. The smell's unbelievable. And people are sleeping and eating in there. So now you see what I mean!

Saturday, 30th November

Yesterday evening Shirl told me that one day, when we were in Wales, the Germans dropped a delayed- action bomb down towards Catford. They cordoned off the area, but before the Bomb Disposal team could arrive, it exploded and demolished a row of terraced houses. (No one hurt, luckily.) Back in Lewisham half an hour later, it was raining feathers in the town centre. The rumour started to go round that a chicken factory had caught it, but really it was only bedding from the terrace up in Catford! Any excuse to laugh, these days!

Wednesday, 4th December

Mum tipped me the wink that Dad's boss wants to put him in for a commendation after what happened in Birmingham. It sounds like Dad was a bit of a hero on the quiet. It's just typical that to have heard him you'd have thought he did nothing at all.

Frank's written to say that he won't be able to get leave at Christmas, but he can spend the weekend after next with us. Hooray! So we'll just have to celebrate Christmas *twice*, won't we?

Friday, 6th December

I went window shopping at Chiesman's yesterday. I haven't a clue what to buy anyone for Christmas, mostly because I haven't the money to buy anything nice.

And the way it is in England right now, you feel bad about spending anything on frivolous things anyway. There's posters everywhere telling you about the "Squander Bug", making you feel guilty if you're not giving your money to help buy another new bomber, or putting it in the bank so the government can use it.

I saw a brilliant green bus conductor's set in the toy department. Two years ago, Tom would have loved it, but he's grown up too fast. Anyway, five shillings and eleven pence is too much for me. Even a new football's three and six, and I can't afford that.

If Shirl can get me the wool, I've still got the time to knit Mum something warm, and I'll work on old Lineham to see if I can wangle some of Dad's favourite pipe tobacco out of him. Mum's given me the OK to make a collage of family photos for Frank. I'll mount them and overlay them so he'll have something he can put beside his bed to remember us by.

Thursday, 12th December

Mr Lineham's a funny old stick. I asked him about the tobacco for Dad's Christmas box yesterday and he tapped his nose and said, "No problems, young Edie. We'll see Mr Benson all right for Christmas, you and me. Man like Mr Benson deserves a little respect and recognition." Then he turned and asked, as if it was an afterthought, "What are you giving young Thomas?"

I shrugged, and said honestly that I didn't know if I could afford much. Then blow me if he didn't fetch a few soldiers from the back of the shop, similar to the ones Tom had nicked, wrap them in tissue paper, put them carefully in an old shoebox, and give it to me.

I didn't know what to say, and stuttered an inadequate thank you.

"Don't mention it," he said. "You're a bright girl, and a good worker. It's just a little something to show my appreciation."

Well I never!

Saturday, 14th December

Frank's home! And he looks so well. I'd swear he looks tanned even though it's December and near freezing. All that fresh air must be doing him good. Over tea he announced that he's going to apply to train as a pilot, and I saw Mum's face fall. Dad asked calmly if he thought he stood much chance, and Frank said what with all the pilot losses there'd been during the Battle of Britain, he thought there was *every* chance. He says he's been thinking about flying every day for the past eighteen months – eating, drinking and sleeping it. It's just that he hasn't actually been *doing* any.

I don't know what to think. On the one hand I can see the glamour of it all. There's this idea that it's very dashing to be a pilot, and all the girls will think you're wonderful. On the other hand, Frank's nice and safe if he stays as ground crew. I read somewhere that once you're trained as a fighter pilot, your life expectancy's three weeks. I just hope and pray Frank's either very sensible or very lucky.

He brought me a very beautiful, very grown-up blue and green silk scarf. It's daft really, because I haven't got anything to wear it with. He just looked at me and smiled and said, "It's your colours. You'll find something." Then he gave me a big hug. I think he was really touched with my collage of photographs, and I know he meant it when he said he thought of us every day.

Monday, 23rd December

For a few days now Tom and I have been out collecting. There's a party for the homeless kids in the Red Cross Centre out at Deptford tonight, and we've been after toys that we could wrap up to make some sort of Christmas presents for them. We've not done too badly, and Dad's knocked up some trucks and boats out of the spare wood he keeps in the shed. They look all right once they're painted up.

Mum was home this afternoon, and she and I made a huge cracker from paper Shirl conned out of the management up at Chiesman's. It's about four foot long, and we've put lots of the smaller toys inside. The Red

Cross van's coming round to collect the cracker and us in a few minutes!

I know they've decorated the hall so that it looks quite festive, even if it still smells a bit "off". We'll have some singing and dancing, and I think they've got a Charlie Chaplin film and some cartoons to keep the kids amused. The Christmas tea might not be all that wonderful, but I think they've managed a cake of sorts. When those kids get hold of it, and there are about 40 of them, you can bet it won't last long! Happy Christmas, Deptford!

Wednesday, 25th December

Last night we went to the midnight service at St Matthew's. As we walked down to the church the air was crisp and cold, and the sky was clear and starry. There was a bomber's moon, but everything was quiet. Even Germans celebrate Christmas! When the bells rang out, and the vicar was talking about "Peace on earth, goodwill to all men", it was very odd to think of people in Germany doing exactly the same thing.

If they say they're Christians like us, how come they've been bombing us to pieces these last few months? I thought of everything we've been through, and I said thank you to whoever it is up there that we're still in number 47, and not homeless like those kids out in Deptford. And I made a big wish that Hitler would get the message and be happy with what he's got and leave us alone.

Before we sang "Hark the Herald Angels Sing", the vicar made a point of saying it was a German tune, and that we had to pray there could be peace with justice soon. As I looked around the church it was obvious not everyone was singing. Mum and I weren't the only ones with tears in our eyes.

Monday, 30th December

Uncle Bob keeps the Lord Wellington pub in Webber Street near London Bridge. He's Dad's older brother and we don't see him very often. He joined the Auxiliary Fire Service early in the war. Dad says Bob saw which way the wind was blowing and thought that if he was called up Auntie Doris would never be able to run the pub on her own. This way Uncle Bob can keep an eye on things. Dad and Bob get on well, but generally there's a funny relationship between regular firemen and auxiliaries, like the regulars think the auxiliaries aren't proper somehow.

Anyway, yesterday Dad piled us on to the bus to spend the day with them. There haven't been any air raids in a while, and we took our night things and toothbrushes thinking we'd stay over.

They're both big, jolly people. Uncle Bob always wears a bow tie, quite often a spotted one, and just to look at her, you'd *know* Auntie Doris worked behind a bar, all bosom and behind. Uncle Bob is the *only* person I know who calls my dad "Albert".

We'd had a lovely day in their living room, high above the chatter of the bars, talking and playing board games (mostly Tom and me) but then the siren caught us unawares when it went off half an hour or so after blackout. Dad and Bob looked at each other, put down their glasses of Guinness, and resignedly went off to do their duty.

Bob and Doris have done the cellar up quite nicely, and I shouldn't think there are many places safer in the whole of London, but we were down there hours and hours and bored silly by the time the all-clear went. We heard, or rather felt, the occasional dull explosion, but nothing to indicate what had really been going on outside. The walls of the Lord Wellington must be very thick.

When we went upstairs about midnight, Doris went to the window and cried out softly, "Oh my Gawd!"

From the big picture-windows of their lounge, you can see across the railway and the River Thames to the City of London. St Paul's sits in the middle, surrounded by all the great buildings belonging to the newspapers and the banks.

It's a wonderful view, so good you feel you should be paying to look at it.

But now the light thrown back from the fires raging across the beautiful city was as strong as the electric light in Bob and Doris's lounge could have been. The shells of at least two of Sir Christopher Wren's churches stood out clearly against the black sky, lit from inside like torches as the flames burnt away 300 years of history. Even at that distance you could see sparks shooting into the air, so powerful was the force of the blaze. The whole panorama was silhouetted in red, like a mad sunset. It made you understand the terror Dad and Bob must face every time they go out to work. The city was being destroyed before our eyes, a second Great Fire of London.

This afternoon, before we left for home and Bob had dragged himself back to the Lord Wellington (blackened and bruised after a twelve-hour shift), the fires were still burning. And you can be sure the bombers will come back for the kill tonight.

Thursday, 2nd January 1941

I don't know quite know how to write my diary today. I'm so full up I could burst. Words won't do any more. I thought

I could get rid of my fear and unhappiness by putting it on paper. Now I know that, when it comes down to it, there are some things you can never tell.

Frank's dead. We had a letter this morning saying so. It must have been the same raids we'd seen from Uncle Bob and Aunt Doris's flat.

I suppose the Germans were softening up the RAF stations to keep our fighters out of the air. Then they'd have had a free run at the city. As if it matters. Everyone knows our boys are no good after dark anyway. They just can't see the bombers well enough, despite the searchlights.

Anyway, according to Frank's commanding officer, some German planes got through to Biggin Hill and strafed the runways. Frank and two other men were out there, desperately trying to get some Hurricanes ready to fly. A petrol tank went up. And that was it.

I thought he'd be safe if he stayed on the ground. I thought death was something that happened to other families. I thought this year would be better than last. God, I don't believe in you, not if you take away the life of someone like Frank who never did anybody any harm. It's not fair. It's so awful, sometimes I catch myself thinking it hasn't really happened at all. How on earth will we ever recover?

Saturday, 4th January

Mum had to go to the undertaker's this morning to make arrangements for the funeral. I went with her. It was a bitingly cold morning under a steely grey sky, so our bodies were as numb as our minds, despite being wrapped up as much as possible in scarves and gloves.

It was a fair walk right up towards New Cross, and I don't know why but on the way home we wandered down through Crofton Park. We were walking along a row of terraces when this woman with her hair in curlers rushes out of her house.

"You've got to help," she says. "She's started. What are we going to do? I can't believe it. How can she have started now? She's not due for another month."

Mum calmed her down, and we went inside. The house was in a right state. I should think it hadn't been cleaned in a month of Sundays. On the sofa in the front room was a girl who didn't look much older than me, groaning and screaming by turns – having a baby. I mean, I've never seen anyone give birth before, but I didn't need telling.

To spare the gory details, it was all over in about half an hour. I didn't know it could be that quick! By the time the doctor arrived he'd missed the arrival of a beautiful new little baby boy. Well, as ugly as a shrivelled prune actually, but who's going to tell a new mother and grandmother that?

And then I made the connection between a birth and a death, and for the first time since we had that letter three days ago I couldn't help myself and I was in floods and floods of tears that just wouldn't stop coming. Soon I was shaking and I couldn't have spoken even if there'd been anything to say.

Friday, 18th April

I know I've been bad and I haven't kept this diary going, but in the weeks after Frank's funeral I just couldn't find the energy. I couldn't see the point in much at all to be honest. The people who'd left Lewisham during the back end of last year have begun to drift back, and I've started to go to a school that's running (mornings only) near Lee Green, so I suppose, what with everything else, my time's been pretty well occupied.

And (until Wednesday) life had been what passes for normal these days. On the whole it's been quiet these last few weeks. The sirens go pretty regularly but compared with before Christmas, there's not been much damage.

On Wednesday the warnings went in the mid-evening, about eight o'clock, and we settled down in the Anderson as usual. It's all right in there now. There's even electric light, though you have to be careful you don't trip over the cables.

You don't often hear the droning of the planes like we did that day. They seemed unusually low and concentrated. Then suddenly out of the blue, there were two almighty explosions. The Anderson and the earth around us seemed to bend and change shape almost before we felt the hollow whoosh of noise that surrounded us and caught us up. Earth was flying everywhere, the lights went out, and then there was the sound of splintering wood and glass. For one awful moment I thought we were going to be buried alive.

Mum was in there with us. Dad was on duty. In the ominous quiet that followed the explosions, she asked anxiously, "Everyone all right?" and though we were all shivering we all said we were.

"What do we do, Mum?" squeaked Tom in panic.

"Hold still," she said. "Who knows if Jerry's finished? Until we know he has, we're safer here."

In fact the all-clear sounded quite soon, but when we crawled out of the shelter and looked back towards the house, number 47 wasn't there any more, and neither was Bessie Andrews's house next door. As we stood there we could already hear the fire bells ringing down the road and, by the time we'd picked our dazed way across the rubble to the street, a fire tender (with Dad clinging on to the side) was dodging the bricks towards where the front gate had been. Mum ran to the tender and she and Dad clung to each other, while we kids looked on not knowing what to do.

In the cold light of day, there wasn't any good news. Bessie must have been in the house next door when the bomb struck. The only consolation is she wouldn't have known anything about it. We'd never been able to persuade her to let the council put in a shelter of her own, or to come and share ours.

When they told us it was safe to go on the site, we wandered about sifting through the remains of our old life. It's funny the way the bomb has utterly destroyed some things, and left others almost undamaged. Take the kitchen for instance. The furniture in there just seems to have vanished, but I found a cup and a saucer covered in dust but otherwise completely untouched – not a chip, not a scratch.

And then there was my diary. By the new year it had filled three exercise books, which I'd kept in a square biscuit tin in my room. Now, as I wandered about on the bricks and fallen beams, I almost fell over the tin, dented but in one piece.

It's a miracle! I don't know why but clearly it was meant to survive along with us. So having made this last entry, I'll keep the diary with me to bring us good luck in whatever comes next. We might need it!

Postscript
April 1946

Five years on, and I've been re-reading what I wrote in that terrible autumn and winter, a time that now seems so very far away.

We *didn't* find ourselves living in the Red Cross Centre after the collapse of the house in Summerfield Road, as I remember being afraid we might. We were luckier than most. Dad's friends at the Fire Station saw us all right, and though we were cramped up together in a poky flat for about a year afterwards, at least we didn't have to leave Lewisham.

Shirl moved straight in with Margaret, a friend from Chiesman's, which was sensible but a bit of a shock for me at the time. As of last October she's become Mrs Goodfellow, and her husband, Christopher, works for Wray's in Downham. They manufacture lenses for the cameras that go in reconnaissance aircraft. He's very clever, and obviously thinks the world of Shirl.

Maureen's still in the forces and says she might make a career out of it. We saw less and less of her during the last couple of years of the war, but she seems happy. To be honest, we don't have much in common.

Tom's a nice lad now. He's taller than me and still growing fast. I don't know where he gets it from. He's got himself a first job down the river at Vickers, near Erith. It's a bit of a bus ride, but I think he thrives on the independence. Somehow I don't think he'll be at home for long. Good thing, too: he takes up too much room! When I look at him he sometimes reminds me of Frank.

Dad didn't come out of the war well. All the years of inhaling smoke and soot have gone to his chest, and he's been invalided out of the Fire Service. These days even gardening's a struggle, which for a man of 51 is ridiculous. For what he did in Birmingham he received a George Medal, a distinction very few firemen in London achieved during the war. To this day he's never talked about the exact details. So he got to meet the King a second time, and reminded His Majesty that the previous time they'd talked about the weather.

"Did we?" said the King. "And what was it like that day?"

My mum goes from strength to strength. Dad says there's no stopping her. In a funny way the war gave Mum an opportunity she didn't have before. If there'd been no war, maybe she'd have spent the next ten years being a housewife, looking after us kids, cooking and cleaning. Being an ARP warden gave her a taste of how good she is at organizing people. She works for Lewisham Council now, and she's on her second new job in a year.

Chamberlain still lives with us in our new house just off Lee High Road. He suffers badly with his nerves after all the bombing, and I shouldn't think he'll ever really be right again. But I'm so glad we didn't have him put down, even though we'd thought about it long and hard during the Blitz. He's far too precious.

Me? I'm a real bookworm these days. I want to go to university to study history, and then maybe politics. This Second World War we've lived through has left most of Europe ruined. We've got to rebuild it, and make it better than it was before. And somehow we've got to ensure there's never a third war, because now we know that if ever there *is*, no diary and no person is likely to survive it.

Historical note

The First World War (or Great War) ended in 1918. By the 1919 Treaty of Versailles, Germany was prevented from re-arming, and made to accept responsibility for all the damage caused by the war. Germany's pride was badly dented, but more than that, the Treaty of Versailles meant a lot of hardship for her people over the next ten years.

Hitler seemed to be a man who could give Germany back her pride, and as he came to power in the 1930s he promised to make her wealthy again. His National Socialist Party, the Nazis, were concerned to make Germany great. They weren't too worried about the morality of the means used to achieve this.

In Britain, the governments of the 1930s watched what was happening in Germany with anxiety. On the whole they thought that a strong Germany would make for a safer Europe. They admired German spirit and technology: they didn't *want* to see the violence that Hitler was unleashing. So they stood by while Germany re-armed and created a powerful air force, and then as it swallowed up Austria and Czechoslovakia. This became known as the policy of "appeasement".

Gradually it was realized that even at home Hitler was using extreme force against groups and nationalities he believed were making trouble. Later, Hitler's bizarre ideas about the superiority of the German people were to lead to the deaths of millions of Jews and others in concentration camps.

In 1939, the British government, led by Prime Minister Neville Chamberlain, eventually decided that a line had to be drawn. They told Germany that if Poland were invaded, a state of war would exist between Britain and Germany. On September 1st, German troops entered Poland, and two days later Britain declared war.

German air tactics were well-known by now. They used dive bombers to terrify ordinary civilian populations, to weaken morale and create panic, making ground operations by their army more effective. So when war was declared, the British people expected German bombers overhead immediately, and indeed on that very first day of the war the air-raid warnings sounded in London. But no bombers came. Not yet.

It was also expected that the Germans would use poison gas, so everyone was equipped with a gas mask, even the very youngest children. In the event no poison gas was used anywhere in World War Two.

Neville Chamberlain was never going to be the strong war leader Britain needed, because he was seen as one of those who had appeased Hitler. Winston Churchill had always opposed concessions to Germany. He wasn't without his faults because he was hot-blooded and always likely to make errors of judgement, but he was a daring and inspirational leader with great vision and a gift for public speaking. He became Prime Minister in May 1940 at a point when Germany had just overrun Holland and Belgium and was about to defeat France. Now, with the United States shying away from declaring war, Britain stood alone.

Invasion by Germany seemed inevitable, and in May 1940, with many able-bodied young men "called-up" into the armed forces, the Local Defence Volunteers or "Home Guard" was formed to help defend Britain.

In July Hitler began to lay his plans. His air force, the Luftwaffe, had always been so successful in the past that most of his military actions on the ground had gone more or less unopposed. He believed the same might be true this time. At first he attacked shipping in the English Channel with great success, halting all convoys through the Straits of Dover. Then, during August, he started to attack the British fighter bases in southern England. The losses of aircraft and men on both sides were great, and if he'd continued with this tactic Hitler might have destroyed British air power completely. But he was distracted into retaliating for the first British night bombing-raids against Germany. He called his planes away from the airfields, and told them to bomb London. He hoped to win complete air superiority, and crush Britain's morale. In the event he achieved neither objective.

For 57 consecutive nights from September 7th 1940, Hitler's planes raided London. Londoners called this the **Blitz** after the German expression **Blitzkrieg**, which means "lightning war". Given the length of time the bombing went on, perhaps this wasn't quite the right word! After London, most other British cities came in for similar bombardment during the period up to May 1941, some – like the centre of Coventry – being almost completely devastated.

More than three and a half million homes were destroyed, often by incendiary or fire bombs. The House of Commons was left in ruins and even Buckingham Palace was damaged. Ordinary life stopped almost completely. About 30,000 people were killed in the Blitz, half of them in London. Up to September 1941, Hitler had killed more British civilians than fighting men. In Lewisham there were over 2,000 fires between September 1940 and May 1941. More than 20,000 incendiary bombs fell in Lewisham, and a further 2,000 packed with high explosive. Nearly 1,000 people were killed here alone. To put it another way, about one in fifty of the average war-time population of the borough was killed or seriously injured.

But the spirit of the British people in Lewisham and elsewhere wasn't crushed, and having failed to find an opportunity to invade in September 1940, Hitler never got another chance. The tide of the war slowly turned against him, although it took until 1945 for the allied armies to reach Berlin and the bunker where he committed suicide.

The story of Edie Benson and her family may read like a fairy tale, but Edie might have been your grandma. These things are not so far away as they seem. . .

Timeline

Sept 3 1939 Britain declares war on Germany.

May 9 1940 Winston Churchill becomes Prime Minister.

May 27 1940 British troops are evacuated from Dunkirk, France.

June 22 1940 Most of France is under German occupation.

July 10 1940 "Battle of Britain" begins.

July 16 1940 Hitler makes plans to invade Britain.

Aug 25 1940 British planes bomb German towns including Berlin.

Sept 7 1940 First "big raid" on London by German bombers.

Sept 17 1940 Hitler abandons invasion "until further notice".

Oct 12 1940 Hitler cancels invasion for winter.

Nov 2 1940 Last of 57 consecutive night raids on London.

Nov 14 1940 Major raid on Coventry leaves city in ruins.

Nov 1940–April 1941 Raids on most major British cities.

Dec 29–31 1940 Devastating air-raids on the City of London.

Apr 16–19th 1941 Some of the worst raids of the war in Lewisham.

May 1941 Hitler turns his attention to Russia. The Blitz is over.

Dec 7 1941 Japanese aircraft attack the American fleet in Pearl Harbor, on the Hawaiian island of Oahu. The US enters the war.

June 6 1944 D-day. Allied troops land in Normandy.

1944–early 1945 V-1 "doodle-bug" and V-2 rocket attacks on London.

Feb 14 1945 As many civilians killed in a single British air-raid on Dresden as in the entire German "Blitz".

May 7 1945 Germans unconditionally surrender on all fronts.

Aug 6–9 1945 Atomic bombs are dropped on Hiroshima and Nagasaki. The world enters the nuclear age.

Sept 2 1945 Official celebration of victory over Japan.

During the war many Londoners used underground stations as air-raid shelters. This picture was taken at Piccadilly Circus station.

Many children were evacuated from London during the Blitz. Some were sent to relations who lived in safer areas, but many were sent to complete strangers.

Soldiers, Civil Defence workers, and civilians search for survivors among the ruins of a bomb-damaged school.

King George VI and Queen Elizabeth made many visits to the
bombsites during the war.

The London Rescue Squad pulling a survivor out of the rubble.

Firefighters in the City of London, December 1940.

A National Service recruitment poster.

ARP wardens had to patrol the streets and report back on bomb-damage and casualties. They were expected to give first aid and help rescue survivors. They also had to make sure the blackout and other wartime regulations were being observed.

Anderson shelters being delivered to a street in Islington. The shelters came in pieces and had to be assembled by the householder.

Picture acknowledgments

P 127   (top) Using the Underground as an air-raid shelter, Popperfoto

P 127   (bottom) London evacuees, Popperfoto

P 128   Searching for survivors in the ruins of a bomb-damaged school, Popperfoto

P 129   George VI and Queen Elizabeth visiting a bombed-out building, Popperfoto

P 130   London Rescue Squad in action, Popperfoto

P 131   Fire fighters in the City of London, December 1940, Popperfoto

P 132   National Service recruitment poster, Mary Evans Picture Library/Explorer Archives

P 133   (top) Air raid warden, Popperfoto

P 133   (bottom) Anderson shelters being delivered to houses in Islington, Popperfoto